# The Dog
# at the Window

HELEN GRIFFITHS

# The Dog
# at the Window

Holiday House / New York

© Helen Griffiths 1984
First American publication 1984 by Holiday House, Inc.
Printed in the United States of America

Library of Congress Cataloging in Publication Data

Griffiths, Helen.
The dog at the window.

Summary: A lonely young girl develops such an intense
attachment to a neighbor's dog that everything and everyone else in her life takes second place.
[1. Dogs—Fiction]  I. Title.
PZ7.G8837Do  1984   [Fic]    84-3806
ISBN 0-8234-0527-3

# The Dog
# at the Window

Alison was on her way home from school, the Union Jack bag with her books inside weighing heavily on her arm. It was a hot afternoon in April, the sort of afternoon that wakes up a memory and makes you start longing for summer. It made Alison start counting how many weeks till the holidays came – not till the end of July. An eternity! Better not count. It was too depressing.

The top two buttons of her white blouse were undone; the green and yellow striped tie was loose, its knot somewhere round her neck; her white socks were wrinkling down to her ankles once more. She'd given up trying to keep them up.

Miss Hobbs, the headmistress, would have gone all red and tight-lipped at the sight of her, meandering home. '*Not a credit to the school*.' (She liked her girls to look smart right to the end of the day. Alison never even started out smart.)

Every morning she just flung on her clothes, which were usually half on the floor and half over a chair. It took her five minutes every day just to hunt down her shoes which she always kicked off within minutes of arriving home – sometimes in the kitchen, sometimes in her bedroom, or on the settee while she watched television. They were never where she had left them, she was sure of that. Somebody or something always moved them, on purpose to annoy her.

5

Every day Mum would remark with patience that was as aggravating as it was unreal, 'Why don't you put them in the same place? Then you wouldn't have this mad rush, looking for them.'

Mum always put everything away and the biggest battles between Alison and Mum always had to do with putting away and tidying up. Alison maintained that it was silly to keep putting away things you were going to use again any minute. Mum always said that things like coats and bags weren't going to be used again any minute. And, anyway, it only took half a second to put things away.

Mum liked the place to be spotless and, as she was out at work all day, she didn't really have time to keep things as spotless as she wanted.

'It's so easy,' she would explain yet again to Alison. 'I always put things away. So if you just put your things away, too, there wouldn't be anything to tidy up, would there?'

There was nothing to say in reply, unless you agreed, so Alison said nothing. But inside her head she would be trying to explain how it didn't work like that. Somehow things got out of place by themselves.

The fact was that Alison and Mum were exact opposites. Alison liked being at home, curled up with a book, as happy on the floor as in the armchair; and she liked a cosy untidiness around her, a 'lived-in' feeling that only a certain kind of untidiness could create.

Mum wanted her home to look as though she'd just bought it lock, stock and barrel from the Ideal Home Exhibition. She was always buying glossy magazines that showed you how you could do fantastic things with colour schemes, or wicker work, or mirrors; and whenever there was any money to spare she bought an ornament or some fine glass – really expensive things. You wouldn't catch her buying half a dozen sherry glasses in the market.

6

'Real cut glass. That's the thing,' she told Alison, having dragged her round several chinaware shops just before Christmas because she'd decided to give a sherry party for her friends. And she spent thirty pounds on half a dozen sherry glasses, which Alison, at the time, thought was quite ridiculous.

Alison was thinking all these things now because she was coming up the hill to the council flats where she lived. She lived in the second block and had to pass the first, the one with the dog at the window.

Every day the dog was there. When she went down the hill on her paper round at seven o'clock it was there, nose against the glass, three storeys up. When she came back three quarters of an hour later it was still there, looking as if it hadn't moved. At half past eight she went down the hill again, on the way to school. She would stop and look up at that third-floor window, and there was the dog. When she came home in the afternoon it was still there.

Did it ever move away? Was it real? Or was it just a stuffed head which someone had put there for a joke? (You could never tell. Some weird people lived round there.) It moved so little that Alison couldn't be completely sure.

Her heart went out to him (or her), stuck there day after day, with nothing to do but look out of the window. She used to stop sometimes and, if nobody was about, she would wave, hoping that those still, blank eyes might see her and show some response. They never did. He just went on staring, black nose pressed against the window pane, smudging it with his breath.

It was this dog that had first made her think about wanting a dog of her own. He was a German Shepherd dog and even on weekends he was always there, staring out of the window, big ears pricked, eyes . . . Wistful? Empty? Dead? Hopeless? It was hard to tell. Sometimes Alison thought they were eyes that saw nothing at all.

She had dreamed about him, until just before Christmas she had said to Mum, 'Can I have a German Shepherd dog?' (somehow hoping that perhaps she would be able to have him). And Mum had told her what she thought of dogs.

At first she had just said they were too expensive (they cost more than the sherry glasses). But when Alison said she wouldn't mind just a mongrel from the dog's home the truth came out. A dog would mess up the carpets, chew and scratch the furniture, and leave hairs all over the place.

'It's not as if we live in a house with a garden. You can't keep a dog in a flat. It's cruel. It's not right,' she went on.

'But I'd take it out for lots of walks. And I wouldn't let it chew things up, and I'd vacuum every day, honest I would.'

'Huh! I know *your* vacuuming. Two minutes flat, the whole place, not even moving the chairs. And after the first three days that would be that.'

The fact was, Mum wasn't a doggy kind of person. She liked to dress up and go out at night, to a show, to a party, to have drinks with friends. Once she said she wouldn't mind having a Siamese cat, because it would look good – expensive – but when she thought about a litter tray and tinned food (which was awfully smelly and encouraged flies), she bought a china one instead, which sat just inside the front door to welcome you with a frozen, blue-eyed stare of disdain every time you came in.

At Christmas she did buy Alison a dog – a golden labrador made of very expensive china, and it stood on Alison's bookshelf above her bed and looked lovely.

Sometimes Alison pretended it was real. She called it 'Golden Boy' – Goldie for short – and made a little collar and lead for it out of some blue wool. She would pull it along the table and talk to it, pretending to be taking it for a walk. But it was a very unsatisfactory relationship, requiring a great deal of imagination.

The dog at the window was really Alison's dream dog, not Goldie. He was dark, almost jet black, and his ears were huge, stiff triangles, fringed with tan. There was a dignity about him, reminding Alison a little of the Siamese cat in the hall, and yet . . .

What was it that brought a pain to Alison's heart every time she saw him there? Surely he was a prisoner, patiently waiting out his sentence, not knowing how long his sentence would be – life, perhaps? The very thought made Alison shudder.

She didn't know much about German Shepherds, but surely they would need lots of exercise, miles and miles of walking, and lots of fresh air. Even little dogs liked to race about.

It must be torture for him, shut up in that flat. Even the biggest flat must be small for a dog of his size.

She tried to imagine a German Shepherd in their own flat, with its two small bedrooms and L-shaped living room. Every time he wagged his tail, he'd knock something over – one of Mum's precious bits of china probably. There would hardly be room for him to stretch out on the floor. But these practical considerations didn't stop her wanting him, or a dog like him, and now and again – like today – longing and resentment would fill her heart.

A couple of times Alison had mentioned the dog to Mum, but Mum wasn't interested in things like that and her replies showed she wasn't really listening. Once she had heard – when Alison said something about complaining to the S.P.C.A.

'Now you just mind your own business and don't go getting people into trouble. For all you know, there's a perfectly good reason why he sits at the window all day. I expect he likes it.'

9

Mum didn't believe in interfering with the neighbours. Live and let live was her motto. It was the only way life in a block of flats was bearable, she said. Otherwise you'd always be at somebody's throat, or they'd always be at yours.

Mum said perhaps he was a security dog – one of those dogs that walked round factories or warehouses all night long, keeping burglars away. 'If that's the case, then he must get plenty of exercise. And of course he'd be home all day.'

Alison had to admit that this was a possibility, so for a while she stopped worrying about the dog at the window, although she couldn't help thinking he looked sad and hopeless.

But then Uncle Reg (that was Mum's latest boyfriend) said no. You didn't keep security dogs at home. They were too ferocious. They had special places for them – kennels – and special handlers. They weren't house-trained like an ordinary dog, so you couldn't keep them at home.

Alison liked Uncle Reg. She rather hoped he might stay being Mum's boyfriend for ever. She never used to bother with the other ones, probably because she knew they didn't really care about her. They made artificial conversations, gave her money, or brought her sweets, but they thought she was a nuisance. Uncle Reg was different.

He used to come early on purpose when he was taking Mum out somewhere so he could talk to her first. And sometimes they went places together, like the fairground, and the pictures, and the seaside. Sometimes Mum got a bit cross because Uncle Reg talked to her so much.

'Come on. We'll be late,' she chivvied him one day. 'I thought you came round to see me, not Alison.'

'I came to see both of you,' he said, giving Alison a wink. It was the wink that made Mum so mad, and made Alison really like him. It was the wink that made it seem as though he and she had secrets that Mum couldn't share.

The front-door key was on a piece of string round Alison's neck. It was the only way Mum said she wouldn't lose it. After Alison had gone in, dropped her bag against the wall (where it promptly fell over and spilled out her tatty books), she gave the Siamese cat its usual greeting – 'Hello, Cat' – and suddenly remembered Mum wasn't coming home at her usual time that day. There was some kind of 'do' at the agency, to promote cheap travel to sunny Spain, or was it sunny Greece? Alison felt that sunny England was much better right now, not so hot as those other places.

It really was a perfect afternoon. Too nice for staying indoors, especially when Mum wasn't coming home. But where could she go? There were lawns round the flats but the boys played there and you were likely to get hit by a ball, or knocked sideways as they ran past (deliberate or not, it was equally painful). The park was miles away, almost, and the streets would soon be filling up with cars queueing to go home.

She went out and stood on the gallery for a while, watching other kids coming home from school, some going straight home, some hanging about in the doorways. As usual, Jason Harding was selling cigarettes to the kids who couldn't afford to buy a packet at a time. At ten pence each, he made a tidy profit.

The really hard-up kids gave a few pennies each and were then entitled to so many puffs. They were always arguing and pushing each other about because someone had taken more than their fair share of puffs.

Well, she certainly wouldn't go downstairs until that lot had gone. She went back indoors, tripping over her school bag and almost sending the Siamese cat flying.

'Sorry, Cat,' she told it, and made a face to herself as she thought of the homework that had to be done. Perhaps if she did that first, quickly, she'd think of somewhere to go afterwards. But first she'd have a cup of coffee and the bit of cheesecake left over from yesterday. It was in the fridge, ice cold and delicious.

She sat at the kitchen table, thinking about the dog, wondering what, if anything, she could do about him. It was all very well for Mum to say not to interfere, but she hadn't seen him and didn't understand about dogs, anyway, unless they were made of china.

This thought prompted her to go and get Goldie. She stood him on the table, just beyond her cup of coffee, and stared at him, trying to imagine how he would feel, if he was real, about being locked up all day, on his own.

Was he on his own, that dog at the window? Was he always looking out to see when his owner was coming home? That was even worse.

'Gosh, Goldie, what can I do?' she asked the shining, blank-eyed labrador.

The very question made her realize that she had to do something, no matter what Mum said. She wouldn't do anything reckless, like call the S.P.C.A. – at least, not yet. But surely she could do something!

She finished the coffee, dragged off the hated school uniform and put on some jeans and a T-shirt. Homework was forgotten. She'd go and do something right now.

Once she was downstairs in the street, Alison stopped. Her heart was beginning to beat fast at the very thought of doing something. She wasn't really the 'doing' kind. Mum was always moaning because she preferred to lie around, reading, or just thinking.

'You can be doing something while you think,' Mum insisted. 'Like tidying your room, or washing up. I do most of my thinking while I'm doing things.'

She couldn't make Mum understand that room tidying and washing up were such depressing occupations that thinking dried up at the very prospect. But now Alison was beginning to realize that, if you weren't a 'doing' sort of person you didn't know where to start if you did have something you wanted to do.

'Hi, kid. Come down for a smoke?' It was Jason Harding.

Alison was very tempted to tell him about the dog at the window. She knew Jason liked dogs. He'd once had a fight with a boy who'd been ill-treating a puppy, right outside this block of flats. Someone had called the police because Jason had a wild temper and no one could stop him once he got going. That had been quite a day but, for once, everyone was on Jason's side, except the other boy's family. Even now they were enemies.

She found herself saying, 'Do you know anyone round here who's got a German Shepherd dog?'

'German Shepherd? What's that?' He pretended to talk as if he was thick, to cover his embarrassment at not knowing.

'You know. Those dogs that look like wolves. Alsatians they used to call them.'

'I still do call them Alsatians. Why call them anything else?'

Alison shrugged. 'I don't know. People just do, that's why. It's their proper name.'

'Why?' said Jason.

Alison thought he was trying to be clever, and she turned away with sarcastic expression.

'I mean, why do you want to know?' went on Jason, not caring about her look.

'Oh . . .' She didn't know how to reply, already regretting having spoken to him. All Jason really cared about was making money.

'Well, you did ask, didn't you? Why ask if you don't want to know?'

'It's just that there's this dog. A black one, I think. Anyway, he's got a black face. And he's always at the window. And I never see him around. And I wondered if you had, or if you know who he belongs to.'

Jason frowned and scratched his fingers through his spikey hair which was growing out of a skinhead cut. He wasn't so ugly now that his hair was growing, Alison decided. He might even be quite good-looking one day.

'No,' he said at last. 'Not round here. Which flat do you mean? And anyway, what's it to you?'

'Oh . . . I just wondered.'

They stood staring at each other. Alison didn't know what else to say. She was kicking herself inside for having started the conversation in the first place. She'd stopped talking to Jason when they both left junior school and started going to different comprehensives. Now they had nothing in common.

'Coming out with the gang tonight? We're going roller skating.'

She shook her head. She didn't want to be part of Jason's gang. She didn't want to be part of anyone's gang. Alison was a loner, and that's why people didn't like her. They thought she was a snob. But she wasn't. She just liked being on her own.

She had friends at school but once she was out of the buildings and on her way home at the end of the day, she wanted to forget all about school. She wanted nothing that would remind her of it, and that included her friends. Six hours a day of being bored to death, with nothing to break the monotony except a change of lesson which often meant even more excruciating boredom, was all that Alison could stand.

Once she was on the way home she could start being herself. She could start thinking and planning and feeling, and do what she wanted to do – which was mostly nothing but think, and wonder, and think some more.

Mum said she was lazy, and this would sometimes bring tears to her eyes. It was so unjust. She wasn't lazy. It

14

was just that somehow she didn't seem to fit in with what everybody else did. They only did things because it was expected of them – whether it was working hard at school, or being absolutely defiant, like all those kids smoking. They only smoked because it was the thing to do. They didn't have any minds of their own.

Jason hung around for a minute or two and then went on his way. Alison started walking in the opposite direction, to make sure he wouldn't come with her. Then she went and stood on the pavement opposite the first block of flats. She looked up at the third-floor window. The dog wasn't there! Now what?

'I'll go and ask about him,' she told herself, suddenly inspired. 'I'll pretend I've lost a dog and ask if they know about him. It'll be an excuse for ringing the bell.'

As she turned into the doorway, heart thumping painfully, she thought, 'Maybe no one will be in.' She really didn't know if she would be relieved or not.

Up the stone stairs she went, not noticing the paint peeling off the walls, or the damp patches seeping down from the landing ceilings, because they were exactly like those on her own staircase. And the smell that clung to all the staircases, of too many people who didn't care, or had given up caring, or had too many problems to care about one more thing. Even the sunshine, and the soft warmth of the early evening creeping over the grass and the streets outside, didn't reach in here.

Alison's footsteps and her thumping heart echoed each other.

Now . . . Which door? She was on the third-floor gallery, but she wasn't quite sure how far along the window would be. There were six doors, all painted the same bright blue. On the floors above and below they were yellow, with blue again on the ground floor. It was supposed to make them look cheerful. Mum said that some people had funny ideas.

The sun did reach this part of the building and a couple of toddlers were sitting by the railings, playing with water in a plastic bowl in which they were sailing some boats amid a shipwreck of story books which were half submerged.

Alison had decided that where they were was about where the dog would live. Perhaps it was their dog. Was it any good asking them? She could never understand what little kids said. They had a language of their own.

Alison wasn't used to small children. She didn't know how to talk to them, or even how to smile at them. They were embarrassing things altogether. And these two just stared at her, mouths open, brown eyes inquisitive, heads turning higher and higher as she came closer. She saw that the door was half open and she could hear a woman singing.

That couldn't be the right flat, she told herself. Somehow she felt sure that there wouldn't be any singing where that sad dog at the window lived.

She went past the plastic bowl and a pair of soggy sandals to the next blue door, still followed by two pairs of dark brown eyes. This was awful. Why hadn't she stayed home to do her homework? It was getting more embarrassing every minute.

She tried to just listen at the door before ringing, wondering if she might hear something encouraging, like the singing next door. But there was silence. Almost against her own will she pressed the bell, and jumped back in shock as something heavy suddenly threw itself violently against the other side of the door. A torrent of vicious growls and barks followed.

The door shook. She could hear scrabbling paws, as if the dog on the other side was determined to tear the door down, and she couldn't help but be glad that there was such a solid barrier between them. She stood back, unaware of the sudden fright on her face, unaware of the two little children staring at her with such interest. The dog's barks and growls grew more wild and ferocious.

'Shut up, shut up,' one of the toddlers suddenly cried out, jumping up and running to the door. He banged hard on it with his own fist. 'Bad dog,' he said. 'Shut up.'

He obviously wasn't scared.

His mother came out, wiping her hands on a tea-towel. She looked at Alison and her smile was comforting.

'Mrs Bailey's out,' she said. 'Did you want something?' There was curiosity in her tone.

'Er . . . um. I'm looking for a dog. I've lost a dog . . .' Alison searched desperately for an answer. The one she had planned was slipping away. It was stupid, anyway.

'I only wish it was that one,' smiled the black woman.

'She woke it up,' said the little boy importantly.

'Yes, but she didn't mean to,' his mother replied. She smiled back at Alison. 'You see, once it starts barking it doesn't like to stop.'

'I am sorry,' said Alison. 'I didn't know. I just . . .'

'She'll be back soon. I expect she's shopping. Do you want to come in and wait?'

'No thanks,' said Alison. She felt so shaky she just wanted to get away. The dog was still growling and yelping and banging at the door. Even the letter box was rattling.

'Put your hand in there and you'll lose it,' said the woman, noticing her glance. 'People shouldn't be allowed to keep dogs like that. You lost your dog then?'

Alison nodded, feeling more and more uncomfortable. She wished she'd never come. What had she expected to gain by it, anyway?

'Well, it's not that one.'

'No. Well, thanks very much, anyway.'

'That's all right.'

She watched Alison go back along the gallery. The little

17

boy waved. She wasn't confident enough to wave back, but she forced a half smile to her face. The dog was still barking, desperate to tear her to pieces, or perhaps just desperate to get out.

Alison went back home, cross with herself for having achieved nothing. She didn't even know what she'd expected to achieve, going there like that. Now she wished she hadn't gone.

What a ferocious dog! Probably the people he belonged to were as nasty as he was. They said that a dog was what his owners made him. There was no such thing as a bad dog, only bad owners.

She wasn't even sure any more if she wanted to help that dog. Perhaps Mum was right. There were a lot of weird people round here, and the best thing was for each family to mind its own business.

She made herself some beans on toast, dumped the plate and sticky saucepan in the sink when she'd finished and started her homework. The phone rang. It was Mum.

'Where've you been all this time? I've been ringing for ages.'

'I just went for a walk, that's all. Why?'

'I wanted to let you know I wouldn't be home till late. You know that "do" we were having here? Well, it's going on a bit and we're going out for a meal. I'm on my way now. So I won't be home till latish. You don't mind, do you, darling? There's plenty to watch on TV. You'll be all right, won't you?'

'Yes, Mum. Don't worry. Enjoy yourself. I'll be all right.'

After a few more words Alison put down the phone. She didn't know if she minded about Mum being out or not. She was used to it by now. Mum hated staying in. Although she liked having a smart home, everything shiny and modern, she didn't like being in it. She always wanted to be out somewhere, at the pictures, at a restaurant, going for a ride to a country pub – anything but stay in.

When Alison was younger, she'd had a succession of baby-sitters, mostly girls only a few years older than herself who wanted to make a couple of pounds. They sat and watched TV while she read in bed and fell asleep with the light on. Then Mum decided she didn't need a baby-sitter any more, once she was ten, and Alison breathed a sigh of relief.

Sometimes she wished that Gran was still living with them. When Gran was there she didn't have a baby-sitter. But Mum and Gran had fallen out and Gran had moved out to a mobile home on a caravan site fifty miles away and they hardly ever saw her.

Alison sighed, feeling really fed up. Not because of Mum, but because the dog was still on her mind. She knew she ought to go back. She just knew in her bones that she must, but she was scared. It was really stupid to want to do something that you didn't want to do. She couldn't even explain it to herself.

She wished for once that she could talk it over with somebody. But who? It was no good talking to Mum. She didn't care, and any thought of trouble would have her putting her foot down. There was Jason Harding. She'd already opened the subject with him. But he wouldn't do either. He might think she was interested in *him*. Some hope! Oh, if only that dog would go away and not be at the window any more.

She woke up to her homework again, finding she'd been drawing dogs' heads all over the cover of her English book.

If she went back again, what could she say? Looking for a lost dog was a silly excuse. All the woman would have to say was, 'Well, I haven't got it,' and that was that. No. If she went back, she'd have to have a better excuse . . .

The front-door bell nearly made her jump out of her skin. She called through the letter box, 'Who's there?'

'It's me, Sunshine.'

It was Uncle Reg. She opened the door.

'Mum's not in.'

'Oh!' He looked crestfallen. Then he brightened. 'Can I come in for a minute?'

'Of course.'

'How about a cup of tea?' he suggested, after they'd been polite to each other for a few minutes.

Alison was glad to escape to the kitchen. Although she liked Uncle Reg, she didn't want to like him too much because he might stop being her uncle one day and then liking him would have been a waste of time. She'd probably never see him again. She was sure his time was just about up. Mum had never had a boyfriend for so long before, or even one like Uncle Reg.

Alison couldn't quite tell why he was different from the others, apart from his being nicer to her than they were. The others always ignored her, or talked down to her. Some of them were better looking than Uncle Reg, but none of them had his sort of eyes or his sort of smile. She could imagine him being someone's Dad, but Mum said he wasn't. His wife had died only two years after they were married. Alison knew he must have been very sad about it because somewhere in his eyes there was still a shadow of it, in spite of the way his smile warmed and pleased her.

Uncle Reg came into the kitchen. He saw the dirty things in the sink and gave a disapproving chuckle. 'Somebody'll be in trouble if they don't clear that away,' he warned.

'I was just going to do it,' lied Alison.

'I'll do it for you while you make the tea,' he offered and immediately set about washing up, just letting the water drain over the plate and swilling the dirty cups round with

20

his fingers. He didn't bother about the sticky saucepan, though, which was what Alison most hoped he'd clean for her.

She decided to do things properly. She got out the little teapot and two pretty cups and saucers, instead of the mugs and teabags she was going to use. And she put them on a tray with a plate of biscuits, just like Mum always did.

'I say, I say, I am being made a fuss of!' exclaimed Uncle Reg. 'What's all this in aid of?'

'Nothing.'

She wanted to say, 'I'm glad you're here,' but she bit back the words.

Over the cup of tea and biscuits Alison told Uncle Reg where Mum was. Then Uncle Reg seemed to grow a bit embarrassed and quite unlike his usual self as he remarked half jokingly, 'Do you think your mum likes me?'

'She must do,' said Alison, 'or she wouldn't go out with you, would she?'

'No, I suppose not. But . . . I mean, I'm not her usual sort of bloke, am I?'

'How do you mean?'

'Well, your mum likes to enjoy herself, doesn't she? Go dancing, and that sort of thing.'

Alison nodded.

'And I don't,' confessed Uncle Reg. 'I take her. I mean, that's what she wants. But sometimes I wish she liked to stay in a bit more. You know, sit at home and just talk.'

Alison nodded again, feeling very sorry for Uncle Reg because he looked as though he was aching somewhere inside and knew neither how to hide it, or how to explain.

'Do you think your mum would ever marry me?' he suddenly said.

'She's not the marrying kind,' said Alison, not meaning to be as brutal as she sounded. It was just matter-of-fact.

21

Mum was always saying that she liked to be free. She was always telling Alison not to get married either – not that Alison, coming up to her thirteenth birthday, had marriage in mind.

'What do you think about it all?' Uncle Reg suddenly asked. 'I mean, wouldn't you like your mum to get married?'

'I don't know. I haven't thought about it.'

This was true. Although she had sometimes dreamed of having a dad – and quite often day-dreamed about her real Dad whom Mum never talked about – Mum had never come anywhere into these dreams. It had been her and a dad, doing things together, like going to the park, boating on the river, or queueing up to buy icecreams – things that she saw other girls doing with their dads. And that's why she liked Uncle Reg so much, because she'd done all those things with him.

But, except when Gran had lived with them, when Alison was much smaller, there had never been anyone but her and Mum together and she couldn't somehow imagine a dad actually living with them under the same roof. Dads were somehow open-air sort of people, for taking you out and doing things with.

She couldn't explain all this to Uncle Reg, although he was looking at her as though he could see what was going through her mind. He smiled and got up, putting his cup carefully on the tray.

'Never mind,' he said. 'I expect it'll all sort itself out. Somehow.'

It was a forlorn sounding word that 'somehow', the way he said it.

After he'd gone, Alison was suddenly miserable. More than miserable, she felt as though she was weighed down, hurting with loneliness. She didn't know if it was hurt for Uncle

22

Reg, who somehow she'd just failed, or hurt for that dog at the window that she'd failed as well.

Perhaps she was hurting for both of them, and for herself because she didn't have any real friends, and didn't know how to make them either. She always drew back, telling herself it was better to be independent, to have a mind of her own. But sometimes . . .

Suddenly, Gran came into her mind. She could never think of Gran without remembering that last terrible argument between her and Mum, when they'd really screamed at each other and said horrible things. They'd both cried, and Alison had cried, and Gran had packed her things the next day and gone away. And the flat had been dreadfully empty. Mum had hugged her and said, 'Never mind. It's just you and me now. It's better like that, isn't it?' And Alison had nodded, too bewildered to understand.

Even now she didn't know if it was better – just her and Mum. They were good friends. Mum was always saying so, even when they did argue about tidiness. But Mum had other friends, too, and Alison didn't.

Goldie was still on the kitchen table. She picked him up and carried him back to her room, staring into his dark, china eyes. Sometimes those eyes looked warm and real, and she almost expected him to bark and wag his tail, but just now they were quite empty, because she was remembering the stare of that dog at the window.

Throwing Goldie down on the bed, she turned and ran out of the flat, slamming the door, dashing down the stairs, not stopping till she was on the pavement in front of where the German Shepherd dog – Alsatian – lived. She looked up and – yes, there he was, at the window again, ears pricked, eyes staring, nose smudging the already much-smudged glass.

Alison was breathing hard from running so far. She didn't normally run anywhere – not even on the school playing field if she could avoid it – but today she was all stirred up inside, what with the dog and Uncle Reg and the sunshine. Even the sunshine somehow made her restless. She liked grey days best. They didn't disturb her.

Again her heart thumped abnormally as she went up that staircase to the third floor. This time she had no plans in her head, no words to say. She'd just ring the doorbell and see what happened. She didn't care any more.

The toddlers had gone, though the bedraggled books that had been shipwrecked in the water lay there as a reminder. This time Alison was prepared for the ferocious response of barks as she rang the bell and it didn't startle her, though she still drew back instinctively.

Growl, yelp, bang – door and letter box shaking. Was nobody in? Alison angrily bit her bottom lip. Then she heard a voice.

'Get out of the way, dog. Go on, move over. Who is it? Who is it? What do you want?'

It was a woman's voice, and not young. Tired, complaining, annoyed. Alison didn't reply. What could she say, anyway?

It sounded as though woman and dog were struggling to be first at the door, the dog yelping to get out and tear the caller to pieces, the woman only half-heartedly trying to stop him.

'Who is it?' she called again without opening.

'It's me,' shouted back Alison. 'Can I talk to you a minute, please?'

'What about?'

Desperately Alison replied, 'The dog. It's about the dog.'

'Oh . . . Wait a minute. I can't hear what you're saying. Get out of the way, Wolf. Can't you see somebody wants to come in? Hang on,' she shouted to Alison. 'Ill just get the

24

dog out of the way.'

The invisible struggle went on, Alison aware that the dog only unwillingly allowed himself to be dragged away. She heard a door slam shut, then the owner of the moaning voice return.

She was a thin woman, with streaky grey hair escaping from pins, defensive brown eyes, and lips with a discontented droop. At a glance Alison took in enough to make her wish she hadn't come – the jumble-sale clothes, ill-fitting and grubby; mauve, fluffy slippers gaudily mocking bare, bony feet and legs; cigarette burning between stained, yellow fingers.

'Well?' There was a certain amount of surprise as well as suspicion in the word.

'It's about the dog.'

'Well?'

'I . . . I just wondered about him. I . . .'

The dog was still barking and yelping and banging against a door.

'You come to complain?' came the question wearily.

'No. Oh no. I . . .'

'What then? Oh, shut up, Wolf,' she suddenly turned and shouted.

Wolf barked even more in response. Alison couldn't help smiling in sympathy at the woman's obvious inability to manage him.

Perhaps something in that smile made a difference.

'Here. Come in a minute,' the woman said next. 'He'll shut up then. It's only 'cause he wants to get out. He's not a bad dog really. It's just his way. Don't worry. He won't hurt you. I won't let him out.'

She said all this while leading Alison into the living room. Alison was glad she was behind the woman because she couldn't help screwing up her nose at the smell of dog and stale cooking and cigarettes. She felt like putting a hand over her mouth. She couldn't breathe and the sun gleaming in through the uncurtained window made it even worse. The room and the smells were baking.

'Sit down if you want to.'

Alison looked for somewhere to sit. There were a couple of colourless armchairs with dirty cushions in them, and some old-fashioned hardbacked chairs round a table which was strewn with newspapers, dirty mugs and overflowing ashtrays. She sat down at the table, trying not to let her feelings show in her face.

'Now,' said Mrs Bailey. 'If you keep still I can let Wolf out. He won't hurt you. He'll rush up and he'll probably growl. But if you don't take no notice he'll stop in a minute, you'll see. But don't go jumping up sudden like. Just let him sniff you a bit and he'll be all right. He's a good dog is Wolf, once you know him. Wouldn't hurt a fly.'

'I'm not a fly.' The vague response fluttered through Alison's head, which was beginning to swim.

Things seemed to be growing more and more unreal until a rushing, growling, wolf-like creature, dominating the room, thrust aside all heat and smell and unreality as he flung himself towards Alison.

He was gigantic, full of fierce strength, and he instantly imposed his will on everything, freezing Alison into utter stillness of mind and body both by his power and his beauty. Back and forth he moved, round and round the chair, growling, thrusting his black nose against Alison's jeans, sniffing her shoes.

'That's right, Wolf. That's right.' Mrs Bailey's voice broke the spell. 'She's a nice girl, isn't she? She's come to visit us. Isn't that nice? Now you just settle down and let her tell us why she's come. He won't hurt you,' she added to Alison. 'See. I told you he wouldn't, didn't I? Come on now, Wolf. That's enough. Sit down with me. That's a good boy.'

After what seemed an age, Wolf seemed satisfied that

Alison wasn't to be torn to pieces. He jumped into one of the armchairs and sat up, tall and majestic, staring at her with dark, intelligent eyes, before relaxing enough to let his long tongue loll out in heavy panting.

Alison had never seen any dog so lovely. He was well named, too, because apart from his black head, and a black saddle the length of his back, he was all silver and grey, just like a wolf. She had seen plenty of black-and-tan German Shepherds, but Wolf's colouring and splendour were something she could never have imagined. He was beautiful!

'Well,' said Mrs Bailey. 'What do you want?'

Alison's mind was quite blank as the woman stared at her, as Wolf stared at her, as the sun and the smell and the airlessness of the room came back and half choked her.

Mrs Bailey didn't help. She just sat in the other armchair and waited. There was a look about her as if she was used to sitting and waiting, to being questioned, to being expected to give answers – and if she hadn't expected the earnest, bewildered, half-choked Alison to be the interrogator, it didn't show. The heavy panting that came from Wolf – sounding like a steam engine straining up a hill – and a bluebottle whining angrily against the window pane were the only things to break the silence.

'Well,' began Alison, feeling hotter and more uncomfortable every second, 'it's just that . . .'

Then, of a sudden, it all poured out, all the things she had been thinking and agonizing over that sunny afternoon and evening. She didn't even know what she said – it all came out so quickly – but she saw surprise, and something else on the woman's face. What was it? Hurt? Indignation?

Somewhat bleakly she ended, 'It's not that I think you don't love him. I'm sure you do. I really do. It's just that . . .

27

Well, he looks so sad there. I am sorry.'

Mrs Bailey pulled a fresh cigarette out of a packet on the floor, having screwed up the stub of the previous one in an ashtray at her feet. Wolf's pants chugged away, occasionally losing their rhythm as he licked round his dripping jaws. His eyes registered every movement Alison made.

Then Mrs Bailey said, 'Most people come to complain about him. I thought that was what you was going to do.'

'Oh no. He's lovely!'

'The people next door. They sent someone round. They said Wolf's dangerous, with kids playing outside and that sort of thing. "What if he got out?" they said.'

'Does he ever get out?' Alison wondered, slightly encouraged because Mrs Bailey seemed to be taking her into her confidence.

'He did once. A while back. He got out and ran off down the stairs. But he came back by himself.'

'And was he all right?'

'He bit someone.'

'Oh!'

Alison stared at Wolf, not knowing what to say. He didn't look vicious. Except for when she'd called at the door and he'd uttered those dreadful threats, she hadn't imagined him being vicious at all.

Wolf's dark, almond-shaped eyes met her gaze, as if he knew what questions were going through her mind. There was no friendliness in them. They were alert, suspicious, but calm. He seemed to be sizing her up, just as she tried to do the same with him.

'Some boy tried to catch him, didn't he?' volunteered Mrs Bailey. 'At least, that's what they said.'

'Who?'

'The police. They called the police, didn't they? People round here are always calling the police. They're always

28

going on about how much they hate them, but the smallest thing and they're on the phone to them. Not about important things, mind. Only about getting people into trouble.'

'And did you get into trouble?'

Mrs Bailey made a scornful sound. 'I don't take no notice of them.'

'But what did they say?' Alison couldn't help being anxious.

'Oh, something about having an order on him. I don't know. I don't listen. They said once more and that's it.'

'How do you mean?'

'What I said. If he bites one more person, they'll take him away. They'll have him put down.'

'Just because he did it once!' Indignation blazed in Alison's heart. 'And maybe the boy had frightened him and maybe Wolf didn't really mean to bite him!'

'Yes, but there was the time before, wasn't there? They got a note of that one, too. When he bit the copper.'

'He bit a policeman?'

Alison was beginning to feel troubled now. What was she letting herself in for? Perhaps it was just as well that Wolf was kept in, locked up. Perhaps he wasn't a nice dog at all. And yet . . . in spite of his watchfulness every time she wiped the sweat from her brow, or moved in the chair, she didn't feel threatened or afraid.

'It was *his* fault,' said Mrs Bailey.

'Wolf's?'

'No. The copper's. He came to take my Bobby away, didn't he? He put his hand on him and Wolfie went for him.'

'Bobby?' said Alison. Was this another dog?

'Bobby's my grandson, isn't he? Wolfie belongs to him. He's been his dog since he was a little puppy. He won some money once, on a horse, and he bought Wolfie with it. He's always wanted a big dog, ever since he was little.'

For the first time a bit of warmth had crept into Mrs Bailey's voice, and her eyes weren't so hard and empty.

'Cost him sixty quid! You think of that. That's what Wolfie cost. And he was so little you wouldn't think he'd be worth it. But my Bobby, he said he was worth six hundred, six thousand. He really loved him. He used to take him out. He was out all day with him, wasn't he?'

Alison was trying to picture Bobby in her mind. She wondered if she knew him, which school he went to. Perhaps Jason Harding knew him. But, betting on horses? Surely you couldn't do that if you still went to school? Unless Mrs Bailey had put the money on for him. Alison didn't know anything about betting. She felt a bit embarrassed about asking where Bobby was now. It sounded as though he might be in prison, if a policeman had come for him.

'Even so,' she found herself saying to Mrs Bailey, indignation relit within her, 'you can't blame Wolf for biting someone who wanted to take his owner away.'

'That's what I said. I told him what would happen. I said you keep your hands off my Bobby or that dog'll tear you. He didn't take no notice, did he?'

'Then it was his fault.'

'Yes, but . . .' Mrs Bailey shrugged, the hopeless look coming back to her eyes. 'You can't tell them that, can you? They don't want to know. They tell you what's what. And they said if Wolf bites one more person that's it. They'll take him away and he'll be put down. And how can I tell Bobby that? It'll break his heart. That dog's the only thing he loves.'

'When's he coming home?'

'That's just it, isn't it?'

There was the strangest look in her eyes that Alison didn't understand at all. For a moment she and Mrs Bailey had shared something. Alison had forgotten that she was only twelve and that this woman was years and years older, grey-haired and bitter. But, suddenly, that look brought her back, made her unexpectedly think of Uncle Reg, made her realize that grown-ups were full of mysteries, secrets, pains, that they didn't or couldn't talk about.

She wanted to get up and run home. All this was too much for her. She didn't want to be involved. But because she was quite unable to just get up and dash out, she found herself inquiring with forced politeness, 'Is it?'

'I don't know when they're going to let him out,' was Mrs Bailey's gloomy response. 'If they ever will.'

'What do you mean?'

Alison was growing frightened. What had Bobby done? Had he murdered someone?

'Well, they've got him locked up in one of them places where they give you treatment. And when you're better, if you're better, they let you out. But there's no date on it, is there? It's not like a prison sentence, is it? Six months, a year. Even a life sentence. You get out after that. But when it's just when you're better, it might be never.'

Her voice, which had risen with resentment, drooped in despair.

'What's Bobby done?' Alison asked, though she was almost scared to know.

'Nothing really. Little things. He used to pinch bottles of milk. For Wolfie. Sometimes. When he was little. He'd be out all day with Wolfie, see, and Wolfie would get hungry and Bobby'd see these bottles of milk on people's doorsteps. He'd only take one. He wasn't really stealing. He only wanted to give Wolfie something to eat.'

'But they wouldn't put him away for stealing a bottle of milk!' exclaimed Alison hotly.

'He sat in someone's car once. He didn't drive it. He didn't have the key to turn on the engine. He was only pretending. You know. For Wolfie. He told me about it. He didn't mean no harm. He was just pretending to Wolfie that he was taking him out in the country. He was always telling Wolf he'd take him out in the country, wasn't he? He lived for that dog, I tell you. Everything he did was for Wolfie.'

Wolf knew Mrs Bailey was talking about him, or about Bobby. His big, triangular ears kept twitching and turning; his eyes seemed suddenly to come alive. Unexpectedly, a little whine escaped his throat.

He jumped down from the chair and went over to Mrs Bailey. He sat in front of her, put one paw on her lap and began to wag his tail across the rug, whining.

'Oh, go away, dog. I can't do nothing for you,' she cried impatiently, pushing his paw off her lap, dropping cigarette ash over herself at the same time but not noticing.

Wolf just plonked his paw back on her lap again. Another little whine, almost a yelp, escaped him. Then, as if all this had happened many times before and he no longer expected any result, he turned, jumped back into the chair, opened his jaws and began panting again. His breath chugged hard and endlessly in the airless room.

Alison felt as if she was drowning. There was something wrong with the whole evening, in spite of the sunshine and the feel of summer in the air. The dog's miserable face, then Uncle Reg, and now this weird tale which was somehow choked with the airless, hopeless smell of the room she had trapped herself in, was all too much for her.

Needing to be able to identify, even if only vaguely, with this boy who loved his dog so much; needing to have something real to hang on to, Alison found herself asking, 'How old is Bobby?'

'Well . . .' Mrs Bailey seemed reluctant to speak. 'It depends what you mean. Bobby's about twelve really, in

32

some things, anyway. I mean, the things he does. The way he thinks. Like playing in the car, and taking the milk. Kids are doing it all the time, aren't they?' she appealed to Alison.

'They do worse things, don't they? You read about it in the papers. Much worse things. And my Bobby's never done anything like that. All he wanted was to be left alone with his dog.'

She had forgotten Alison now. This was an old argument. She'd been over it before, perhaps a hundred times. Perhaps with other people, perhaps on her own, thinking things out. Perhaps even talking to Wolf.

'But people wouldn't leave him alone. They're always making fun of him. And he doesn't understand, see. Not most of the time, anyway. Sometimes he does, though, and then he gets angry. Once he had Wolfie, they left him alone. They wouldn't tease him with Wolfie around.'

'Is he a bit . . . a bit . . .?' Alison couldn't bring herself to finish the question.

'He's slow. If people left him alone, if people didn't expect things of him, he'd be all right. He's nineteen now and he's a lovely boy, really. He's always been good to me. And if you just leave him to get on in his own way, he's happy. Like having Wolfie.'

Mrs Bailey suddenly saw the ash on her skirt and rubbed it in, a hint of pride in her voice as she went on, 'He trained him all by himself, you know. Ever so well trained he is. He'll do anything my Bobby tells him. But you got to do what people expect. And if you don't, then they start wanting to change you. They won't leave you alone. They come along with smiles and everything, but they're hard as nails underneath. It's got to be *this* way because They say so, and the minute you say no, then you see what they're really like.'

Alison wasn't sure what Mrs Bailey was talking about,

but she could feel the bitterness in her towards the mysterious 'They' who wouldn't leave her and Bobby alone.

'Hasn't Bobby got a mum?' she found herself asking.

'She went off years ago. Left him with me, didn't she? Wanted to enjoy herself.' There was no anger, no resentment. All Mrs Bailey's anger, what was left of it, was reserved for 'Them'.

'Do you go and see him?' Alison asked next.

'Yes, but all he says is, "Where's Wolf?" He wants his dog there. He'd be happy if he could have his dog, but he can't, can he? It's against the rules. And you can't break rules, can you?'

'And won't they ever let him come home?' Alison asked incredulously. It sounded like some kind of nightmare.

'They want to help him. They've got some kind of work shop. They said they'll decide, when he's settled down. He gets a bit violent sometimes. But it's only because they won't let him have his dog. I tell them that, but they say I don't understand. They use all them big words. They don't know what they mean themselves.'

'And what about Wolf? Do you take him with you when you go to see Bobby?'

'I can't take him out. He's too strong for me. I don't know how to manage him. I'd never get him on the bus. And even if I could, I expect they've got rules about it. They'd probably say it'd upset him – you know, seeing Wolf. And it would. But I talk about him, and he likes that.'

Mrs Bailey suddenly looked at Alison as if she were seeing her for the first time. Surprise, doubt, suspicion chased one another across the lined, sullen face.

'Why'm I telling you all this, anyway? What's it to do with you? You're only a kid. What you come here for, anyway? You still haven't told me.'

Her stare was unnerving. It took all Alison's reserves to

34

get out the words, 'It's because I want to do something for Wolf.'

The dog seemed to open his eyes wider as she used his name. He lifted his big, proud head a little higher, full of disdain. Alison's heart went out to him. How easy it must be to love a dog like that, so beautiful. Surely he understood every word.

'What can you do? What can anyone do? If it wasn't for Bobby's loving him like he does, I wouldn't keep him. I can't afford him. You don't know how much he eats. And then the smell. He can't help it, poor animal. I mean, I can't take him out, and he's got to go, hasn't he? But if he gets out and bites someone again, it's the chop, isn't it? And how can I tell Bobby that?'

'I'd like to help look after him,' Alison ventured, heart beating fast again. What was she letting herself in for?

Mrs Bailey just stared at her. Alison didn't know what she was thinking.

'Couldn't I take him out? I'd be ever so careful with him. I'd never let him off the lead. I wouldn't give him the chance to bite anybody, honest I wouldn't.'

'He's a big dog. He's like a horse. Strong. You don't know. He'd pull you over, he would. I tell you, it's no joke with a dog like him.'

'Didn't you say Bobby had trained him?'

'Yes, but that's Bobby, isn't it? You're not Bobby, are you? Why should Wolf do what you tell him? He don't know you, does he?'

'But he's so lovely,' cried Alison. 'He needs to go out. He needs lots of fresh air and exercise. He needs to be groomed and . . . and – well, everything. I'd be ever so careful with him,' she pleaded again.

'I can't pay you, if that's what you're thinking. I haven't got any money. People have offered to buy Wolf off me. I had a man only the other day. Offered me twenty quid for

35

him. He's got a pedigree, you know. This man wanted to breed from him. Says he's a good dog.'

'I don't want to be paid!' exclaimed Alison, interrupting her. 'I just want to make him happy, that's all. He's always at the window, and he looks so miserable.'

As if not hearing her, Mrs Bailey went on, 'Sometimes I think it might be a good idea. Not for the money. What's twenty quid? He cost my Bobby sixty. But, I know something's going to happen one day. He'll get out, or I'll get ill. And sometimes I don't think Bobby'll ever come home. He used to be independent, but he isn't any more. And he's only been there six months.'

'Please don't sell him,' begged Alison. 'Not yet, anyway. Bobby might come home. And then what?'

Mrs Bailey sighed. She pulled another cigarette out of the packet. The matches were under the chair and she fumbled round for them, and lit up again, before answering.

'You can't take him out,' she said. 'Not yet, anyway. Not till he knows you. But you can come here if you want. See if he gets to like you. Then we'll see.'

Alison jumped up with an exclamation of joy. Wolf sprang out of the chair at the same time, lunging towards her menacingly.

'Wolf!' yelled Mrs Bailey as Alison froze to the spot. 'He don't mean nothing,' she went on. 'He's all right.'

Wolf sniffed round Alison's legs. She felt his nose pressing against her jeans. Her heart was thumping madly from the shock of his sudden spring, but she slowly bent forward to run a hand along his back.

Wolf turned on her, making her jump again. All his movements were as sudden as they were graceful. Alison's hand froze in mid-air, which was perhaps just as well. Had she snatched it away, she felt he might have gone for her. As it was, he sniffed at her fingers, black nose slow and deliberate.

He knew he was frightening her. He knew he had her in his power, as a snake hypnotizes a rabbit, and he was glorying in it. Low growls came from deep inside him, undisturbed by Mrs Bailey's commands for him to be quiet.

'Hello, Wolf,' Alison forced her stiff throat to utter.

It was no good pretending she wasn't frightened because Wolf knew just how fast her heart was beating. She'd just have to try to make friends on his terms, not her own.

He went from her fingers to her arm. Then he sniffed at her T-shirt and paced all round her once more, silvery grey tail waving slightly as he grumbled inside like a restless lion. Then he jumped back into the armchair and stared at her again, regal, proud, confident that he had put Alison in her place.

'Can I stroke him a minute, before I go?' Alison asked.

'He won't take no notice,' Mrs Bailey said.

Alison didn't care. Her heart had stopped racing wildly. She wasn't *really* scared of Wolf. She told herself that if Bobby could love him, then she could too. And if he could love Bobby, then he had a good heart in spite of his record.

Oh, it would be really something to win the heart of a dog like that!

She went over to him and offered him her fingers. When he disdainfully turned his head away, she just let her fingers very gently sink into the ruff round his neck.

'You're beautiful,' she breathed. 'So beautiful. If you were my dog, I'd love you so much.'

Her other hand went up to his skull. She rubbed her fingers along the hard bone, and he didn't seem to mind. He smelled as stale as the room, making her want to wrinkle up her nose, but he was beautiful and intelligent and bold and, to Alison, nothing else mattered. She liked the proud way he sat in the chair and even as she stroked him and said soft things to him, she knew in her heart that one day she and Wolf would be friends.

Mum wasn't in when Alison got home. She wasn't sorry because, just then, she would have had to blurt it all out to her. Normally it wasn't difficult to keep things from Mum. She was always so full of her own affairs that, so long as Alison listened and made the right comments at the right moment, Mum didn't seem to notice that conversations between them were nearly always one-sided.

Alison was quite sure that if she did talk about Wolf, and tell the truth about him, Mum would forbid her to have anything to do with him. Mum wouldn't like Mrs Bailey, and if she saw the state of the flat she lived in . . .! The smell of the place still clung to her and there were dog's hairs all over her jeans. It was a horrible place and, if it hadn't been that Wolf was such a beautiful dog and obviously in need of someone to rescue him from his unnatural existence, Alison knew she would never go back.

In spite of everything, Alison had returned home happy. She hadn't expected to win Wolf over in five minutes but at least they knew each other and that was a start. Mrs Bailey had said she could come and visit Wolf whenever she liked.

'But I don't suppose you'll get anywhere with him,' she said cheerlessly. 'He only puts up with me. He don't love me, not like he loves Bobby. Still, you can try.'

That was enough for Alison. She told herself she would go round to Wolf's house every afternoon, on the way home from school. Mum need never know. She didn't get back from work till about six.

Alison went to bed, but she couldn't sleep. She was too full of plans for herself and Wolf, too full of all that had happened that evening. She heard Mum come in at last. She called out softly, 'You awake, Alison?' A pause, then, 'Alison?'

Alison didn't answer, too wrapped in her own thoughts to want to hear about Mum's evening out.

So many questions kept filling her head which she just couldn't answer. The biggest question was, what could she really do about Wolf? She knew she wanted to have Wolf love and obey her and be with her, the way he had been with Bobby. She knew she wanted to be able to roam about with him, suddenly realizing there were all sorts of interesting places to explore when you had a dog to keep you company – places that you just wouldn't bother about on your own.

Uncle Reg had a car and some weekends they'd have a picnic in the country. The country started about only a mile from home. You could see it from the flats – wood-covered hills, green fields, grazing black and white cows. Uncle Reg said there were all sorts of places round about you could walk to, without using the car, but Mum didn't think much of walking.

'Oh, let's get away from here,' she'd always exclaim impatiently, when Uncle Reg suggested walking somewhere. 'Who wants to stay around here?' and they always did what Mum wanted.

Sometimes Alison had thought about exploring those not very distant woods and fields, but Mum wouldn't let her.

'You can't go on your own. There's too many weird people about these days. Somebody might attack you.'

'Who's going to be up there?' Alison protested.

'That's just it, isn't it? Nobody, but perhaps you and some nut-case. And it won't be any good screaming because there'll be nobody to hear you. Now, if you went with a group of friends, that would be different.'

Friends! Alison didn't know anybody, except Uncle Reg, who would like to walk through fields and woods. All the people she knew just wanted to go into town and spend their pocket money on records, or clothes, or nail polish. They wouldn't even walk to the shops, but had to get a bus.

But with Wolf for company . . . Surely she could go anywhere with him. A big dog like that, who would bite anyone that tried to hurt her! She'd be safe as safe.

Wolf was the beginning of a whole new life for her, if only she could make friends with him.


Lessons at school next day were completely wasted on Alison. She dreamed her way through them, unnoticed by the different teachers. They were happy if someone in the class just kept quiet, so they didn't disturb her. She pulled out her rough book to copy the evening's homework off the blackboard, and underneath started the list of thoughts and questions that kept going round and round in her mind. Perhaps writing them down would help her see things more clearly.

1. When will I be able to take Wolf out?
2. Will he be safe? Will I be able to control him?
3. Suppose he bites someone?
4. What's the best way to make friends with him?
5. How will I know if he's safe to take out?
6. Suppose I take him out and he runs away and gets lost?

She didn't write all these questions down at once, but added to the list as they came into her mind. Throughout the day the list grew.

7. Suppose Bobby's gran never lets me take him out?
8. Buy a nice brush and comb for Wolf if he hasn't already got them.

40

9. Try and keep him clean.
10. Has he got a collar and lead? Find out how much they cost. Go to pet shop on way home.
11. What if Wolf doesn't like me?

She put down the last question because it was something that really worried her. She had read various dog stories, and they were always about dogs that only loved one person and wouldn't have anything to do with anybody else, however much that person loved them. If Wolf only thought about Bobby – the way dogs in stories always seemed to think about their masters – she wouldn't stand a chance with him. Oh well, she'd find out soon enough. And she wondered about Bobby, too, locked up because he didn't fit in with the way most people did things.

On the way home from school that afternoon she wondered whether to go to the pet shop first and find out about brushes and leads, or whether to go straight to Wolf's. Already she was getting a sick kind of feeling in her stomach as she thought of seeing Wolf again. She was a bit scared of him. She couldn't pretend she wasn't. She longed so much to have him love her . . . She hated Mrs Bailey's flat . . .

One feeling after another surged around inside her. In the end she decided to go straight to Wolf. Surely once she was with him all these horrible feelings would disappear.

She saw Wolf at the window as she came along and her heart leapt. If he saw her, he made no sign. He seemed to be lost in his staring, looking at nothing in particular. If only he knew how much she longed to save him from that prison . . .

She felt all warm and good inside because of what she wanted to do for Wolf, and she ran up the stairs and along the gallery, suddenly cheerful and hopeful again.

She rang the bell, grinning to herself at the expected barks and the body flung against the door, making the letter box rattle. She called through the door to him, 'It's me, Wolf. It's me!' but he just went on growling and threatening.

Nobody shouted at him. Nobody came. Nobody stopped him. Biting her lip, Alison rang again, making Wolf start up his furious barking once more.

'Oh do shut up, Wolf. It's me. Me. Don't you remember me?'

He stopped. Was he listening to her? Was he remembering her? She tried to imagine him beyond the door, ears pricked, eyes questioning, perhaps even an eagerness to have her with him to break up his loneliness.

The letter box was suddenly tempting. Could she look through it? Could she see him? She pushed her fingers through, then drew them back with a jump of fear as Wolf gave a ferocious growl and snapped at her, crashing against the door once more. Alison felt the sweat break out all over her.

She didn't dare ring the bell again, or touch the letter box. Wolf was more or less quiet, though she could hear him snuffling at the foot of the door.

She thought, 'If he could get out, he'd tear me to pieces!'

The letter box rattled again, as Wolf tried to get his nose through it.

Alison was determined not to give up on him. She'd talk to him through the door if she couldn't see him. Surely sooner or later he'd get to know her? Surely he would be able to tell by her voice that she wanted to be friends with him? So she started a one-sided conversation with him, because there was no one around to make her feel a fool.

'Wolf? Wolf? Can you hear me?'

42

Silence.

'I know you're there. I know you're listening.'

She heard his claws on the floor. He was moving around. Was he listening? Were his ears pricked?

'Wolf, don't you remember me? I came to see you yesterday. Have you forgotten me already?'

Bang on the door! Alison could just imagine one paw hitting out. She remembered how he had planted one paw on the woman's lap, asking, demanding, going away unsatisfied.

'What are you doing, Wolf? I do wish I could see you. I do wish you'd be friendly.'

Silence. But he hadn't gone away. Dare she try opening the letter box again? No . . . It wouldn't be a good idea. Where was Mrs Bailey? Had she forgotten all about her? Was all her dreaming and hoping and planning just a waste of time? Would she and Wolf never be friends?

Alison suddenly felt as though it was all useless. She had been kidding herself, dreaming again, as she did with Goldie. She would never have a dog of her own, especially not a dog like Wolf. She was mad. He was ferocious. He'd bitten two people. He'd run away with her the very first time she took him out. Why didn't she just go home and forget about him? If she had any sense she would.

Even as these thoughts went through her head, she remembered how lovely he was . . . That silvery grey coat, just like a real wolf's; that intelligent black face; that sense of grace and power in every movement.

'Oh, Wolf,' she cried in near despair. 'Things could be so good for us if only you'd try to understand!'

Wolf made a funny little sound, half bark, half yelp, not a bit threatening, more like an answer to the cry from her own heart. The sound came again, the paw slammed against the door again, and then came a whole chorus of yelpy barks that stirred Alison to the depths.

'Let me out, let me out,' those barks seemed to say. But she couldn't let him out. There was the door – and a whole lot of other things to prevent her.

Time after time Alison went back to Mrs Bailey's flat to see Wolf, and each time the only reply to the bell was Wolf's wild threats. He was on his own. Mrs Bailey was out. A couple of times she saw the next-door neighbour, or the children, who stared at her with disconcerting curiosity. They would watch while she rang the bell, fascinated by Wolf's response. Much as Alison wanted to talk through the door to Wolf, their unblinking stares drove her away.

When no one was there, Alison stayed much longer, trying to keep Wolf from going away. At first he hardly listened, padding away just as soon as he knew who it was and had lost interest. But, on the Thursday evening, when once again Mrs Bailey was out and Alison felt like crying with frustration and disappointment, Wolf didn't go away.

Barking, grunting and sniffing over, silence fell, and Alison could almost feel Wolf on the other side of the door, waiting for something to happen. She could almost see him listening, head slightly to one side, dark eyes alive.

Almost breathlessly, she said to him once more, 'It's me, Wolf. Don't you remember me?'

This time, when he barked, it was an entirely different sound. It was an answer, a definite 'hello' as if at long last he recognized that Alison was somehow connected with him.

'Oh, you lovely boy,' she called to him. 'You lovely, lovely boy.' The tears that hadn't been so very far away almost overwhelmed her. But now they were prompted by relief and joy.

Wolf barked again, that sharp, deep sound with a little yelp in it that so tugged at Alison's heart. Then she heard his nose sniffing at the letter box, and a heavy thump against the door as if he was trying to get out. A volley of demanding barks followed, not threatening, not ferocious. Just the barks of a dog longing for company, longing for freedom, frustrated by a locked door.

Alison kept talking to him, forgetting about time, forgetting where she was, putting all her heart into the words, so much longing for Wolf to recognize and accept her. Now and again Wolf barked back, but suddenly this conversation was rudely interrupted by a man who came out of the door on the far side of Mrs Bailey's, a newspaper dangling from his hand.

'If that dog don't shut up, I'm calling the police. What do you think you're up to, anyway? Causing a disturbance, you are. Go on. Get out of it. You don't live here.'

His tone was so threatening, his looks so unpleasant, that Alison didn't have the courage to argue. She just stared at him, shocked, then hurried away, tears smarting in her eyes.

Half way down the stairs she stopped, hardly able to breathe, chest hurting. Just then, if Wolf hadn't already become something very special to her, she would have decided never to go back. The whole thing was too much for her, too much effort, too hopeless, too unpleasant.

Then anger against the man for his violent outburst overcame her. Why did people have to be so nasty? Why couldn't they just put up with each other? Alison suddenly became just a little bit more aware of Mrs Bailey's problem. Everyone was against both Wolf and Bobby and people's way to solve problems seemed to be just to get rid of them by passing them over to one authority or another. Bobby was locked up, and everybody wanted to have Wolf put down.

Alison's fighting spirit wasn't very strong. Till now, she hadn't really found anything worth fighting about. So much of her time was spent in her own little world of books or make-believe that not very much happened to disturb her. When there had been the fight between Mum and

Gran, Alison had shrunk into herself and kept out of it, unable to take sides, shutting them both out of her heart until one of them was gone. At school she minded her own business. When an argument arose, she kept her opinions to herself, rather than let her feelings betray her.

It was a safe and comfortable little world most of the time, hardly disturbed since last Christmas when she had wanted a puppy so badly, and got Goldie instead. Even then, after a few tears in the bathroom, successfully repressed, and an ache in her heart which had eventually faded, Alison had conformed once more to reality, inwardly bolstered by her dreams.

But now Wolf, who had begun as a kind of dream – just a dog at the window who was hardly real – was breaking up that shell of hers. In just a few days her whole world was turned upside down.

Alison still shook all over, standing on the dank stairway, but she was shaking with anger and determination. Fright was gone. She'd take on the whole world to save Wolf if she had to. She wasn't going to give up, no matter what anyone said. She'd show them. She'd show them. She hardly knew who 'they' were, except that surely even her mother would be one of them, as much as that horrible neighbour and those who had locked up Bobby. Instinctively, Alison ranged herself against them all.

On Friday night Mrs Bailey was in. She didn't give any reasons for not having been home before, even though Alison told her she'd called several times.

'I suppose you've come to see Wolf?' was all she said, in a tired sort of way. Ash dropped down the front of her cardigan as she took the cigarette from her mouth.

For once Wolf hadn't come running to the front door. He was shut up in Bobby's room where he barked and banged. It seemed to Alison that there was a certain amount of anticipation in his barks. Surely he recognized her voice?

'Can I go in to him?' she asked eagerly, determined not to let Mrs Bailey's apathy dishearten her.

'Better not. I'd better let him out. Once I know he's all right, then you can do what you like. I don't want no more trouble with him.'

She said this quite resentfully, as if she expected Alison to make trouble, as if Alison's interest were already another burden.

Wolf charged out as soon as she opened the door, all black and silver flowing lines. He did his usual circling round, threat rumbling in his throat, long tail waving, nose pushing hard against Alison's legs. Alison stood like a statue, thrilled at the sight of him, sure too that behind his threats there was a certain welcome.

He was more beautiful than she remembered him, although she'd been thinking of him constantly for days. She'd forgotten how powerful he was. Even though she was sure he wouldn't hurt her, she couldn't keep her heart from beating as he took charge of her, took charge of the whole room.

She put out her hand to him as she called his name, but he completely ignored it. He remembered who she was, he recognized her voice, but he either didn't understand that she wanted to be friends with him or – worse – he didn't care. Somehow he seemed to melt away from the offered caress, and he padded back to his room.

'It's what I said,' Mrs Bailey remarked hopelessly, but not without a hint of scorn. 'He only wants Bobby.'

'He hardly knows me yet,' returned Alison, refusing to be put off, scared that Mrs Bailey would tell her to go away. She went on eagerly, 'Look, I've brought a brush and comb. Can I groom him, please? I'm sure he'll like that.'

'He's already got a brush and comb. Bobby got them for

47

him. He was always brushing him, Bobby was. Every day. I don't. I can't manage him.'

'Then let me.'

Mrs Bailey shrugged. 'Do what you like,' she said.

Wolf was on Bobby's bed, muzzle on paws, eyes half shut. It was a big bed, under the window, and the faded red eiderdown covering it was screwed up and full of holes nibbled by Wolf in his hours of boredom. The pillows were stained and nibbled too. The whole room smelled of dog and hopelessness. Alison tried not to notice.

Wolf raised his head as soon as Alison came in, looking at her in that regal way of his, dark eyes demanding rather than curious. The way he looked at her made Alison feel as though she'd been called into Miss Hobbs's office for doing something wrong.

'Hello, Wolf,' was all she could say, and they just stared at each other until Wolf switched his gaze to the open door behind her. He yawned, showing brilliantly white teeth, licked his long tongue round his jaws, then looked at her again. Did she just imagine it, or was there just the slightest hint of expectancy in his stare?

Oh, this dog was a challenge. Every movement, every look seemed to tell her so. On the surface he was suspicious, remote. He wanted to bully her, to see how she would react to his bullying. He made out he didn't care, just to see what she would do next. But underneath . . . Underneath, he was as lonely as she was.

And Alison's heart responded. For once in her life she had something real to do, something she wanted to do. She had something real to care about, with no strings attached. She could just be herself with Wolf; prove herself with him; fulfil all the dreams she'd dreamt with Goldie.

Ever since she had bought the brush and comb in the pet shop, Alison had longed to use them. She'd taken them out of the plastic bag several times at home, when Mum wasn't around, to run the soft bristles over her hand. Now she put the bag on the bed in front of Wolf and started to rustle inside it. Wolf pricked his ears, suddenly very curious.

'That's got you wondering, hasn't it?' Alison told him, pleased that for once he wasn't in control. 'What is it?' she went on, grinning at his curiosity. 'It's something for you. Look!'

She pulled out the brush and put it on the bed in front of him. Wolf stretched down his head to sniff at it. She took out the comb and laid it beside the brush. Did he know what they were for?

'What are we going to do, Wolf? Do you like being groomed? I bet you've forgotten what it's like. I'm going to make you the most beautiful dog in the world.'

Alison kept on talking, just wanting Wolf to know how much she cared about him, and it was good to see how he began to respond, how he just couldn't remain indifferent. At first his expression had almost been a replica of Mrs Bailey's – suspicious, apathetic – but as she went on talking to him his eyes were coming alive.

She didn't know how Bobby had talked to him, what Bobby had done with him, but she got the feeling that Wolf was being stirred by old memories – or new hopes. His eyes went from her face to her hands, and back again. His ears moved back and forth. But some uncertainty held him back. Distrust? Loyalty to Bobby? Alison didn't know but, whatever it was, she was determined to overcome it. Even as she talked to him and watched him, she felt more and more confident. Doubts faded. She just knew she could win Wolf's heart.

She picked up the brush and began stroking it along Wolf's back, hardly knowing how to begin. She had never groomed a dog in her life. For a moment Wolf just stayed there, head turning slightly towards his back as if to see what she was up to. Then, suddenly, a sparkle came into

49

his eyes. He jumped up with a short bark, startling her, and bounced over to the chest of drawers near the door, tail wagging, his whole body eager in a way Alison hadn't seen it before.

'What do you want?' she asked, puzzled, but at the same time excited because he was trying to tell her something, really wanting to communicate with her.

He barked again, impatient, expecting her to know. Then he thrust a paw against the chest of drawers. Now she noticed how scratched it was. This was something he had done many a time. With Bobby?

She put down the brush and went over to him. Wolf's long, heavy tail wagged slowly. He put both paws up on the chest of drawers, his nose almost reaching Alison's. Again he barked.

'What is it?' she wondered.

Wolf's paws made a little impatient dance. She put out her hand to stroke his head but he shook it off. Mouth open, eyes sparkling in a way she'd never seen them, he was trying so hard to tell her something she ought to know.

Slowly, uncertainly, she began to pull open the top drawer. Wolf jumped around her, excited, impatient. The drawer stuck and while she struggled with it, Wolf whimpering in a way that made her want to laugh with delight, Mrs Bailey came in.

'Oh, you've found 'em, have you?' she said. 'I told you he had everything, didn't I? Here! Look at the way he's behaving!' she exclaimed, staring at Wolf. 'He knows, you see. Got a memory on him, he has.'

Mrs Bailey struggled with the drawer for a moment and pulled it open. All that was in there, lying on faded newspaper, was a set of grooming tools – a big metal comb, of much better quality than the one Alison had bought; a brush with stiff bristles like a yard broom; a softer one much like Alison's; a hound glove, and a pair of scissors. There was also a short lead attached to a choke-chain collar.

'My Bobby really looked after him,' said Mrs Bailey. 'When he wasn't taking him out he was combing him and bathing him and I don't know what. He was as happy as could be all day long with Wolfie, he was.'

Alison took out the big brush. Wolf was going round and round, hardly able to contain his expectancy. He panted, jaws open in a grin, eyes gleaming. Perhaps a whole train of memories had been sparked off. Perhaps hope had suddenly come back to him.

'He used to stand Wolf on the chest of drawers here. He just used to say "up" and Wolf was up here.'

'Do you think if I say it, he'll jump up?' asked Alison.

Mrs Bailey shrugged. 'You can try,' she said.

Alison turned to Wolf. She patted the top of the chest of drawers. 'Up boy,' she said, hopeful if not confident.

This was what Wolf was waiting for. He obeyed immediately, moving with cat-like effortlessness, hardly seeming to have jumped at all. He sat down and he stood up. He moved round and round, almost slipping off the chest of drawers, too excited to keep still.

'Gosh, Wolf, I didn't know you liked being groomed that much!' laughed Alison. 'But keep still, or I can't do anything.'

He didn't keep still. He jumped off the chest of drawers and suddenly seemed to go wild, pouncing on the bed, thrusting his nose in the bedclothes and grabbing them in his teeth. The eiderdown made a ripping sound as Wolf fiercely shook his head, tail wagging madly.

'Stop it, stop it!' shouted Mrs Bailey, but Wolf took no notice.

He dragged half the bedclothes on the floor, growling all the while and getting himself tangled up in them. Then he

51

abandoned them just as suddenly. He jumped up on the chest of drawers again, threw himself off, out through the door; came rushing back to spring on the bed again, and he barked and barked and barked with a gleam in his eyes that defied all control.

'He's having one of his fits!' exclaimed Mrs Bailey. 'I knew it wouldn't do no good, you coming here. Look how you've got him all worked up!'

Somebody next door started banging on the wall and Wolf turned towards the noise, taking it as a challenge, barking even louder, his lips savagely drawn back.

'It's best to shut him up till he's calmed down. Come on.'

Mrs Bailey grabbed Alison's arm. She was obviously frightened. Until then, Alison had been standing there, grinning at Wolf's antics.

'He's all right. He only wants a game,' she protested.

'You don't know. You don't know. He goes all funny sometimes and there's no controlling him then.'

Wolf sprang at the wall, trying to bite it. His ears were flat. He fell back and sprang forward again, attacking the wall with snarling jaws. Alison allowed herself to be pulled out of the bedroom. Mrs Bailey slammed the door.

'I'll sell him, I will. I can't have no more of this worry, I can't. Oh, shut up,' she shouted at the neighbour who was still banging on the wall.

Alison, bewildered, scared by Wolf's attack on the wall, cried, 'It's not his fault. He needs to get out. Anyone would go crazy, locked up all the time. Please let me look after him. I know I can. We were all right a minute ago.'

'Sit down,' Mrs Bailey almost snapped. 'We'll have a cup of tea. He'll be all right in a minute. He was never like that when Bobby was here.'

Alison didn't fancy a cup of Mrs Bailey's tea, wondering if the mug might be clean, but she was even more scared of being turned out and not being allowed back. So she sat at the table and listened to Mrs Bailey in the kitchen and Wolf growling and snarling in the bedroom and banging against the door, and she felt like crying because only a minute ago everything had been so perfect, and now it had all gone wrong.

She went to the bedroom door and called Wolf's name, as she had done for days. After a minute or two Wolf was silent. She heard him pad over to the door. She heard him whimper. Mrs Bailey was carrying two mugs to the table.

'He's quiet now,' said Alison. 'Can he come out?'

'I don't know . . .'

'Oh, please, Mrs Bailey.'

'Well . . . Sounds like he's calmed down.' She went to Bobby's door, grumbling, 'But I tell you, I'm sick of it. Wolf! Are you going to behave?'

Wolf gave a subdued yelp. It didn't sound a bit like the dog Alison thought she was getting to know. When Mrs Bailey opened the door, he padded dejectedly into the living room and flopped on the floor near Alison's feet. He didn't look up at her. He just put his head down on his paws, and there was a depth of misery in his unseeing eyes that tore at Alison's heart.

Now indeed he was the dog at the window again, all pride and joy and power crushed out of him by so wearisome an existence.

Alison knelt down beside him. He let her stroke his head, uncaring. She wasn't the person he wanted. For a moment she had given him a wild hope, reminding him of his life before Bobby was taken away. But reality was walls, ceilings, a locked door, and a dirty window pane through which to watch a world no longer his.

That evening Alison talked and pleaded until at last Mrs Bailey agreed to let her take Wolf out. It wasn't easy and if

Alison hadn't instinctively felt that this was what Wolf needed most of all, she might not have persisted. Alison wasn't a very persistent person. You have to care very much about something to fight for it, and Alison had always retreated from battles, afraid of her own emotions.

'I can't be responsible,' Mrs Bailey kept on insisting. 'I can't be responsible if anything happens. If you can't control him . . . If he runs away from you . . . If he bites someone . . . I can't be responsible. I can't cope with any more trouble.'

With every 'if' Mrs Bailey was giving way. Alison sensed it, and sensed too that this was how she had let go of Bobby. Surely they had talked and talked to her about him, trying to convince her that it was all for his good, and in the end she had agreed because she didn't know how to say no.

Alison sat on the floor beside Wolf and the mug of tea from which she only sipped politely from time to time. She stroked Wolf's head and put her hand round his neck, losing her fingers in his thick fur. He didn't seem to mind, but neither did he show any particular response. Most of the time his eyes stared nowhere. Was he thinking about anything at all? Did he know what the talk was all about?

'I can manage him,' she kept saying. 'I can manage him. Really I can. I'm used to dogs.'

This was a lie, but only just, because all the time she sat beside Wolf Alison felt closer and closer to him. She just knew in her heart that things would be all right between them if only she could have him to herself, away from everything connected with Bobby. She felt she knew about Wolf, and therefore she knew about dogs. Her confidence soared as her love went out to him.

He sniffed the mug where the tea was growing cold. Alison dipped her finger in it and offered it to him. He ignored it, but a little while later he got up, put his nose to

54

the mug and started to lap. He drank the tea out of it with such skill that Alison knew he must have drunk tea from Bobby's mug many a time.

'He likes his tea,' Mrs Bailey said. 'Do you want another one?'

'No thanks. All I want is to be able to take Wolf out. Please say I can. Please.'

Wolf seemed to have some understanding of her urgent pleading. As he licked the last splashes of tea from his muzzle and jaws, he kept looking from one face to another. And he whined, softly, anxiously, before jumping into his armchair to continue his watch of their faces.

Mrs Bailey looked at Wolf and looked at Alison. Before, Alison had always thought Bobby's gran just looked bad-tempered, but now she saw that she had a weary face, one without any kind of expectation. She was a bit like Wolf when he looked out of the window on to a world that didn't know he existed.

'If things go wrong . . . If he gets lost . . .'

Her voice was like her face and if Alison hadn't been so determined to get her own way, she might have felt sorry for Mrs Bailey just then. Some sort of compassion swept over Alison in that moment, but she checked it hurriedly, instinctively recoiling from caring too much. Caring for Wolf was one thing – she could give herself utterly to him. But Mrs Bailey . . . Well, she was human, anyway. She could look after herself. She wasn't locked up like Wolf. She was free to come and go.

'If anything happens to him, it won't be my fault. If he has to be put down, then that'll be it, won't it? I won't have the trouble of him no more.'

'You mean, I can take him out!' It was a triumphant cry, hardly a question. Mrs Bailey recognized it, even if Alison didn't. But even then she was incapable of giving a final 'yes'.

'It won't be my fault, will it? I've done my best for him. I can't be expected to do more. It's not right for someone like me to have to look after a dog like him. I can't be responsible. It's too much.'

The distress behind those blankly spoken words was lost on Alison, who could hardly believe that she'd won.

'I'll be responsible for him, Mrs Bailey. Really I will.'

She could suddenly feel warm towards the old woman, intensely grateful. But she was thinking of Wolf.

She went home imagining herself in the park with him, throwing him a ball, watching him race about with other dogs he might meet there. But then a kind of fear gripped her heart. What had she let herself in for?

Wolf wasn't Goldie. He was real. Wolf wasn't a little, curly tailed mongrel only knee high and eager to please. He was the biggest dog she'd ever come across and if he chose to run away from her, even on a lead, how would she ever be able to stop him?

From being a person who never voluntarily let herself in for anything she couldn't control, all of a sudden she had plunged into the most impossible adventure of her life. The pictures of playing with Wolf in the park, seeing him bounce back to her with a ball in his mouth, eyes gleaming, tail waving, faded into darker imaginings . . . Of Wolf pulling the lead out of her hands, running away from her, refusing to come back, charging up to some child in the street, frightening him, perhaps attacking him . . .

Alison was home by this time. As usual, Mum was out. She'd gone to the cinema with Uncle Reg. The flat felt empty, lonely. Alison wished she'd stayed longer at Mrs Bailey's. It was a miserable place, but at least Wolf was there.

She knew she only felt like this because she was scared. It wouldn't have made any difference if Mum had been home. She couldn't have told her about Wolf – not yet, anyway. She'd never understand.

Perhaps once she'd made Wolf look really beautiful; once she'd brought a brightness to those deep, sad eyes of his and got rid of his stale, doggy smell; once he was obedient to her and she could have full confidence in him – perhaps then she could bring him home and Mum would see how beautiful he was, and like him because he was a pedigree dog, as beautiful as the Siamese cat in the hall – only better because he was real.

She stroked the cat for a little while. The empty feeling faded as she imagined bringing Wolf home. From just bringing him home, she jumped to imagining him belonging to her properly, living in this flat with them, Mum saying she could keep him, Bobby not wanting him any more.

But Bobby did want him. According to his gran, Wolf was all Bobby did want. If he came out of that place, what then? And if he never came out . . .? They were questions without answers.

Alison decided to make herself a cup of coffee and think about things one day at a time. The big thing was tomorrow. Who could tell what might happen after that?

It was Mum's Saturday at work. She had to work every third Saturday. Usually she grumbled, but just now she was in a really good mood because she had been asked if she would like to go to Greece for a week, paid for by the firm.

'You wouldn't mind, would you, Alison?' she asked. 'You're a big girl now. You could easily look after yourself for a week and I expect Uncle Reg would pop round a couple of times to see you're all right.'

She had never left Alison alone for a whole week before, but Alison didn't mind. All that sprang immediately to her mind was, 'A whole week! I can bring Wolf here, and maybe keep him here for a few days, if Mrs Bailey will let me.'

57

'When are you going?' she asked, almost too eagerly. Mum looked a bit surprised as she buttered her breakfast toast.

'It's not fixed yet. Four or five weeks from now. They're opening a new hotel there, and the agency's been invited to send along a representative – that's me – to get business for them.'

'Sounds fun!' Even as Alison said this, she couldn't imagine anything being more fun than having Wolf all to herself for a whole week. Surely she could persuade Mrs Bailey!

Alison had done her paper round. It was still quite early and she was longing for Mum to go to work. She wanted to take Wolf out before there were a lot of people on the streets, before those little kids next door to Mrs Bailey were out playing on the gallery. She couldn't leave before Mum because she wanted to make some sandwiches. She planned to stay out all day with Wolf, to go right into the countryside with him, to give him a wonderful day, one that he would never forget. But Mum would start asking questions if she saw the sandwiches, so Alison put on her blankest face and pretended to be in no hurry at all.

Mum suddenly said, 'What do you think of Uncle Reg?'

'He's all right.'

Alison was rather surprised at the question. Mum always did ask her opinion of a current boyfriend, but that was usually at the beginning of a relationship, not when it had already been running on for so long.

'Just all right?' Mum sounded a bit disappointed.

'Well, he's nice, isn't he?' Alison's heart was beginning to beat fast. She didn't want to talk about him. She liked him too much.

'Do you like him?' Mum persisted.

'Yes. He's all right.'

Alison's discomfort grew with every question. She and Mum rarely talked about anything that mattered very much. She rapidly started knifing marmalade on to her toast, concentrating hard, sure that Mum was about to tell her that it was over, that Uncle Reg wouldn't be coming round any more.

The sick sensation of pain and panic that she had first felt when Gran went away, and which hit her every time a new man came into her mother's life, was rising up in her, till she remembered what Mum had just said about Uncle Reg popping round to keep an eye on her – and that was a month away!

'Alison! What are you doing with the marmalade?' Mum exclaimed.

She'd piled on enough for three pieces of toast.

'Sorry. I wasn't thinking.' She kept her eyes down, just wishing Mum would go off to work, so she could go off to Wolf.

'He was saying last night that perhaps we could all go away together for a summer holiday this year. You'd like that, wouldn't you?'

Alison's only thought was, 'What about Wolf?' Summer holidays seemed very unreal just then. Only Wolf was real that Saturday morning, and the day they were going to spend together.

'Well?'

'You go if you want. I don't mind.'

Mum jumped up from the table, looking exasperated. 'Really, Alison, there are times when I just don't know what's going on in your head. You're so ... so self-contained.' She made it sound like an insult. 'You read too many books, that's your trouble. You should be out with friends, having a good time, enjoying yourself.'

'I am going out,' Alison was stung into replying. She almost burst out with everything just then, but checked

59

herself in time. Mum would have a fit if she knew.

'I'm going out with a friend who's got a dog and we're going to be out all day, and we're not coming back till this afternoon.' The words came out resentfully.

Mum ignored the tone. She was putting the finishing touches to her hair, looking at herself in the mirror.

'Well, that's good,' she said. 'I'm pleased to hear it. You just enjoy yourself, and I hope you'll be in a better mood when you come home.'

Just as soon as Mum had gone, Alison made herself some peanut-butter sandwiches. In the fridge there were a couple of cold sausages on a plate, left over from last night's supper. She put them in a plastic bag for Wolf, sure that all the walking he was going to do would make him hungry. She'd bought two bars of chocolate at the paper shop that morning, a milk one for Wolf and a peppermint one for herself. Perhaps if Wolf behaved himself on the lead, she could go into the pet shop and buy him some dog biscuits.

As she made these preparations and pulled on her jacket, pushing the bags into her pockets, excitement rose. There was a slight chill of fear at the bottom of her stomach. Did she really know what she was doing? Was it really going to be as good as she was hoping? Was Wolf really worth all this anxiety?

Then she remembered how she had seen him at the window, just an hour earlier, not knowing the fun that was in store for him. It was going to be the best day of Wolf's life, hers too. Even Bobby couldn't love Wolf more than she did.

It wasn't easy to get the collar over Wolf's head. He kept leaping up and dancing about, rushing to the door and back again, hard nails clattering on the bare floor. But Alison didn't care because he'd greeted her that morning as if he was really pleased to see her and knew all along that she was going to take him out.

Mrs Bailey was still in her dressing gown, cigarette stuck between her lips as usual. 'You'll never manage him,' she kept moaning while Alison confidently replied, 'I will. I will,' determined not to let her change her mind.

Mrs Bailey opened the front door when at last Wolf had the collar round his neck. Alison nearly fell over him as he darted out, the 'goodbye' snatched from her lips as she was dragged in his wake. And from dreaming, Alison was brutally yanked into reality – the reality of Wolf charging with all his strength along the balcony and down the stairs as if completely unaware of Alison at the other end of his lead.

From that first stumbling over him as he shot out of the door, Alison regained neither her balance nor her wits. How she managed to half leap, half fly down the stairs without crashing on to her face she was never to know. It was like the first time Uncle Reg took her on the big dipper at the fair, when suddenly her breath was snatched away, her stomach hit her throat, and her heart didn't beat until the whole thing was over.

There was a blur of rushing steps, battered walls, sharp corners, and a fierce pain somewhere, before – of a sudden – it was over. She was standing still, arm seemingly half out of its socket, and Wolf was off on his own, careering all over the lawns half way up the hill, trailing the lead behind him.

Blood dripped from the fourth finger of Alison's right hand. The tip had been trapped by the clip on the lead and a chunk of flesh at the side of the nail was hanging off. It throbbed intensely, bringing tears that were held back more by the horror of the situation than any sense of stoicism.

'Wolf! Wolf!' she found herself screaming, but Wolf

61

didn't even look back.

He pranced and danced, and chased an imaginary playmate round and round the saplings, then loped off further up the hill to the next bit of lawn in front of the flats where Alison lived.

She began to run after him, heart pounding with anger and fear. Suppose she couldn't catch him? She'd asked herself this when dreaming about taking Wolf out, but she hadn't really believed that it would happen – and she'd never found an answer to the question, anyway.

She kept calling him but he didn't even look at her. How beautiful he was in the sunlight, big jaws open in a grin of delight, tail waving, that graceful, black and silver body revelling in freedom.

Another dog appeared, a brown and white mongrel half his size. As they both stiffened up and then slowly approached each other, tails tentatively wagging, Alison hoped she might be able to get close enough to grab Wolf's lead. But, from the corner of his eye, Wolf saw her intention and bounced away, the mongrel following.

They began chasing each other, lost in a game of their own making, gambolling over the road, between parked cars, back on the lawns again, round and round the trees, never far away but completely out of Alison's reach. What a game it was, and if Alison hadn't been so scared and shaken and desperate, she would have enjoyed seeing Wolf having such fun. She kept calling him but, out in the open, drunk with freedom, Wolf didn't even remember who she was.

The little mongrel darted off down the hill. Wolf overtook him with floating, effortless strides, gambolling right past Alison, almost knocking her over but giving her no chance to grab at the lead. Desperately she followed.

They reached the main road, where a line of traffic sped by in both directions. Alison seemed to shrink inside as they gambolled across, bringing one car to an abrupt, tire-screeching halt. As she ran after them, the driver swore at her. There were people on the opposite pavement who had seen the incident, but no one made any attempt to get hold of Wolf's lead. Alison hated them all just then.

Red-faced, chest hurting, almost crying aloud, 'Please, please. Don't let him get run over,' while not even knowing to whom she made the desperate plea, she followed the two dogs, ignoring the disapproving remarks, though she felt like shouting back bitterly at those who made them.

Just then a boy came out of a newsagent's, just in front of Wolf. Immediately summing up the situation, he grabbed the lead. Alison heard him exclaim, 'Hey, where do you think you're off to?' Then he looked round to see where Wolf had come from. It was Jason Harding.

It could only have been Alison's red face and desperate expression that made him connect her with the runaway dog. He grinned and waited for her to come up, chatting to Wolf in the meantime and stroking his head. Wolf was all over him, dancing about, but not trying to get away. He seemed to have forgotten the other dog, which had disappeared down a side street, and was thoroughly pleased with himself.

Unable to speak because she was so choked with suppressed tears, Alison nodded miserably.

'Didn't know you had a dog. He's lovely, isn't he? Where you going with him? Bet you haven't had him long.'

Alison didn't want to cry, especially not in front of Jason Harding, but she couldn't help it. Dreadful gasps escaped her and the more she tried to hold them in, the worse they sounded.

Jason stared at her, his grin turning a bit awkward with embarrassment. 'Here,' he said. 'No need to cry. I got him for you. He won't run off again. Good boy,' he said, making a big business of patting the panting, tongue-lolling

Wolf, to save himself from having to look at Alison.

Wolf responded with tremendous enthusiasm, slobbering his tongue all over Jason's hands and pawing at him with little yelps of joy. They had a great time together, the two of them, while Alison somehow got her tears under control and began to recover from the shocks of the last five minutes.

'Where you get him from?' Jason asked her. 'Here, do you want him back?'

She shook her head, not yet ready for perhaps a second ordeal.

'I'll walk along with you a bit if you like,' he offered. 'I'm not going anywhere particular.'

They walked side by side, Wolf between them. With Jason he behaved like a perfectly trained dog. Now and again he began to pull ahead, and Jason jerked on the lead and said sharply, 'Here! None of that!' to which Wolf meekly responded.

Alison began to think it was all part of a nightmare. She still couldn't trust herself to speak, but that didn't matter because Jason had plenty to say and didn't seem to notice her silence.

'All you got to do is let him know you're boss. They're all right then. They try it on, you know. We had a dog once. He wasn't an Alsatian, but he was a real beauty. My dad trained him proper. I helped him. He'd do anything. Tricks, the lot. There wasn't anything he didn't know.'

'What happened to him?' Alison found herself asking. Her voice was a bit shaky, but at least she could speak.

'When my dad went off my mum didn't want him. Said she couldn't afford him. He was big. He ate a tin of food a day – one of them big ones – as well as his biscuits.'

'Oh.'

'She had him put down, she did.' The way he said this stopped Alison asking any more questions.

64

They walked along in silence for a while and Wolf behaved as if he was used to padding along between them. His strides were long, smooth and even, and Alison and Jason, without noticing it, were striding along pretty quickly themselves to keep pace with him.

Alison was wondering what she ought to do about Jason, who dressed like a skinhead, was an awful show-off, and wasn't the kind of person Mum would like her to be with. She had heard that he was 'on probation', but she wasn't quite sure what that meant, only that it couldn't be anything good.

'He's well trained,' Jason broke the silence. 'Where you get him from?'

'He's not mine. I'm just taking him out for somebody.'

Jason swore and went on, 'Must want your brains tested, if that's how he behaves with you. Are they paying you?'

'No!' exclaimed Alison indignantly. 'I want to take him out. There's no one else, you see.'

She found herself explaining about Mrs Bailey and Bobby.

'Oh, I know,' broke in Jason. 'He's that dog you asked me about, isn't he? And this Bobby's in the nut-house, is he? Oh, well . . .'

It sounded as if Jason was used to other people's problems and didn't care much about them. Perhaps he had enough of his own.

'Where you taking him then?' was the next question.

'I wanted to take him out to the country. Up to those hills. The ones you can see from the flats.'

'You want to go on your own, then? Do you think you can manage him?'

They stopped and Jason put the lead in Alison's hand. Wolf jumped up between the two of them, big tail waving. Then he plonked his paws on Jason's chest and slobbered over his face. Jason grinned and pushed him away.

'I reckon he likes me,' he exclaimed.

'You can come as well if you like,' said Alison diffidently, not knowing if she really wanted Jason's company or not. Wolf obviously wanted it, and she herself was scared of what might happen if Jason suddenly went off in the opposite direction. Suppose Wolf wanted to go with him, instead of with her? She glanced at her finger, which still throbbed and looked a mess.

'Did he do that?' said Jason.

'Yes. When he ran down the stairs with me.'

Jason's face tightened up as though he was trying hard not to laugh. Then Alison began to laugh, thinking how silly she must have looked, being dragged down the stairs, and the two of them laughed together, Wolf dancing excitedly between them with waving tail.

Wolf settled down surprisingly quickly, although from time to time he jumped up at Jason, asking for attention, and getting it, too. He didn't try to escape any more. Whenever he began to drag, Alison pulled him back, but he didn't take any notice until Jason said in a hard voice, 'Heel!' She said it, too, but Wolf ignored her, which was maddening.

'You don't say it properly,' Jason told her. 'Not as if you mean it. It's no good being polite and saying please. Dogs don't understand that. You got to be firm.'

So Alison tried to be firm. When she was angry enough, because it still didn't work, she brought out the word in a very hard tone and yanked at Wolf's collar. Then he looked up at her with an expression of guilt mixed with reproach, but slunk into place at her side. At first, that look of his made her feel guilty, until she realized that Wolf was summing her up, finding out which of them was going to be boss. And then she laughed, loved him all the more, but grew more confidently firm with him. When Wolf started to take notice of her, it made her feel good.

Within twenty minutes they had climbed a very steep hill, crossed a country road, climbed up to an even steeper field and left the city behind. With grass beneath his paws, and the smell of cows and rabbits in his nose, Wolf became tremendously excited. He looked so beautiful, eyes bright, big ears alert, whole body quivering, that Alison soon completely forgot the dreadful way the morning had started.

It was hard to keep up with him as he tried to bound up the field, sticking his nose into damp holes in the rocky ground, keenly following scent trails. Alison was glad to hand him back to Jason for a while. He was more able to clamber without getting breathless and he didn't mind following the zig-zagging Wolf whose nose wanted to be in six places at once.

But, after a while, even he had to stop to wipe the sweat from his forehead. 'I wish we could let him off the lead,' he said. 'I bet he wouldn't run away.'

'Not yet,' insisted Alison. The road was still in sight and she didn't want to take any risks.

'If we had some string, we could tie it to the lead. Make it longer. Give him more room,' suggested Jason who was looking a bit red in the face.

'Perhaps we'll find some,' said Alison hopefully.

They found some plastic baler twine wrapped round a gate post. It didn't take long to unravel it and, although it wasn't ideal – because it cut into your hand if Wolf, in his eagerness, started pulling – it was better than nothing. Later on, they found some more, to tie to the first piece. So Wolf had at least two extra yards of freedom as they followed the public footpath across the flat fields at the top of the hill.

Even in her dreams, Alison hadn't imagined just how much fun taking a dog for a walk could be. It had to do with the way Wolf so utterly enjoyed himself. He was a completely different dog in the fields. There were so many important things for him to discover and follow up; things to smell, things to listen to, things to watch; that his companions were all but forgotten. He was in a world of his own.

There was the blustering wind that ruffled his thick coat and made him dance and bark, longing to race with it. There was the unexpected swooping bird, startling him; the staring, black-and-white heifers, big eyes curious, suspicious. Some of them half lowered their heads, instinctively remembering a time when nature had given them horns to protect themselves; and Wolf perhaps instinctively remembered a time when his kind had hunted in packs.

He whimpered and trembled, but took notice of Alison's repeated warnings. 'Good boy, Wolf. Leave them alone. You can look, but that's all.' He wanted to chase them, but he knew it wasn't allowed.

Alison had to drag him past the herd. He kept looking back, whimpering, but in the next field they were forgotten as Jason took the lead and went racing ahead with Wolf bounding beside him. Jason fell over and Wolf toppled on top of him. They wrestled with each other, Wolf pretending to bite Jason's arms and legs, and for a moment Alison felt a twinge of jealousy. Wolf was *her* dog, and yet he seemed to like Jason best.

Up in those big flat fields, with a stone wall on one side of them and endless fields on the other, there seemed no reason to keep Wolf on the lead. They discussed it for a little while and Alison agreed to let him go. Wolf dashed off immediately, so fast that it would have been impossible to catch him, and Alison's heart began to pound.

'Oh no!' she couldn't help crying out, but Jason just grinned at her, then turned his gaze back to Wolf.

'He's all right. Just look at him. Having the time of his

life. He'll be back. You'll see.'

Jason was right. After all, he knew about dogs. Wolf used up some of the surplus energy that had been stored up over the past six months by making two great circles round the field at full speed. Then he suddenly made a bee-line for Jason and Alison, jumped up at them both with lolling tongue; dashed off again to complete another, smaller circle, then came back and dedicated the rest of the time to making just short sallies here and there, following scent trails and waiting for them to catch up.

Every now and again he looked back. He didn't forget them. He was obviously glad of their company. And every time he looked back – those dark eyes questioning, hopeful, full of anticipation; that big, black head and silvery body so powerful and majestic – Alison felt her heart swell with love and pride.

She had never known that you could love a dog so much. She had ached for a puppy, she had been very fond of Goldie in a way, but this feeling for Wolf was more real than anything she had ever known. Every time Wolf came back to them, she hugged him to her, letting him slobber his big tongue all over her face as she sunk her nose into his neck. She loved him so hard that it hurt.

Jason's greetings were more offhand. He sort of pushed Wolf away, even while he grinned, and they were more likely to scuffle with each other, Wolf growling ferociously, Jason teasing. It was a different kind of love but, by the end of the day, Alison knew in her heart that Jason cared as much about Wolf as she did.

If she hadn't been so happy that day, this feeling about Jason might have upset her. She wanted Wolf all for herself. She was trying to forget that Wolf wasn't really her dog, that she was only, in a sense, 'borrowing him' from Mrs Bailey in Bobby's absence. When Bobby came back home, if Bobby came back home . . . She shut the thought out of her mind. Just now, it was hard enough not to be jealous of Jason.

They stopped for a rest in one of the fields. Alison pulled the squashed-up packet of peanut-butter sandwiches from her jacket pocket, as well as the sausages and the chocolate. Wolf was there immediately, sticking his wet, black nose into everything, making them laugh even as Alison tried to shoo him away.

'There's not much,' she apologized, offering Jason a share in the battered triangles of bread. 'I brought the sausages for Wolf, but you can have one if you like.'

'No. He can have 'em. I'm not really hungry,' said Jason, but he took half share of everything and gave most of it to Wolf, which didn't please Alison at all.

She didn't mind Wolf having the food. He swallowed it down as if he hadn't eaten for weeks, tail wagging, eyes anxious and pleading, a little whine in his throat as he drooled all over them. What she minded was that Wolf kept going to Jason for everything first. She had planned to feed him herself, to let him know that all good things – walks, company, food, love – came from her. She didn't want to share Wolf with anybody.

She called his name and he came to her eagerly, but the minute Jason called, or even moved, Wolf's eyes were on him. Perhaps it was because he was used to being with Bobby and didn't know about girls. Boys were rougher. They did things in a different way, loved in a different way – in a way Wolf understood. It wasn't fair!

When the food was gone, and Wolf was quite sure there was nothing left, he flopped down beside Jason, panting through half-open jaws, eyes alert, ears pricked. And Alison thought to herself, 'I don't want Jason to come out with us any more.'

Even so, it was quite fun to be with him. He'd given up showing off and talking big by the time they'd climbed up the first hill. In the field, while he smoked and she got up and went to sit on Wolf's other side – to be close to him and let him lick her fingers – Jason told her a bit more about his own dog.

'I hated my mum when she had him put down,' he said after a while. 'And I won't never forgive her. She did it on purpose. 'Cause she was mad at my dad.'

'Do you still see your dad?' Alison wondered.

Jason shrugged. 'Sometimes. He takes me out. But he's got this other family now. And they've got a dog, a labrador. I don't like 'em. They're stupid.'

He jumped up, calling to Wolf and running off across the field. Wolf was after him in an instant, bounding along with such graceful movements that Alison watched him entranced. Now he was nothing like that dog at the window she felt so sorry for. Surely this must have been the kind of life he was used to, wandering about with Bobby? It was cruel to keep him any other way.

They came to a wood, where Jason suggested a game of hide-and-seek with Wolf. They waited until he was distracted, then ran off in different directions, hiding behind trees and bushes. Wolf always found them. Whether it was because he had seen them (he hardly took his eyes off them for more than a moment) or whether he just had a marvellous sense of smell, Alison didn't know. But it was fun being chased by Wolf. Their laughter and shouts, and Wolf's barks, echoed among the trees, making birds fly back and forth in a flurry, and squirrels freeze against the tree trunks.

They came to the canal and followed it as far as they could, till they weren't very far from home. Jason threw sticks into the water and Wolf dived in after them. Even when there weren't any sticks, he threw himself in again, just loving the water. He swam from bank to bank several times, making a swan hiss at him, making passers-by exclaim.

The worst part of the day was having to take Wolf back to Mrs Bailey.

'You've been letting him jump in the canal,' she accused Alison. 'I can tell. He stinks. My Bobby was always bringing him home stinking.'

Alison felt like saying that it wouldn't make much difference – the flat smelled so horribly of cigarettes and dog already. But she didn't want to fall out with Mrs Bailey, and wasn't even sure if she was complaining. Everything she said was a kind of moan.

When she went home Wolf wanted to go with her. He thought he was going to get another walk. Alison hated having to shut the door behind him, to hear him whimper and bark hopefully, listen in silence and bark again when there was no response.

Jason had left her at the flats. He'd said, 'Want to come out with us tonight?' But Alison had said no. She just wanted to go home and dream about Wolf.

Wolf became a changed dog. He still sat at the window every day – Alison saw him when she did her paper round and when she came home from school – but there was a different expression on his face now, as if he were seeing the street outside with hopeful eyes. It was no longer beyond his reach. Perhaps he was even looking out for Alison, waiting for her to come along.

If only Mrs Bailey would open the window. She would shout his name. She tried waving to him sometimes but Wolf never saw her.

It didn't matter. Just as soon as Alison had swallowed her tea, she was off to Mrs Bailey's flat. The evenings were growing longer and there were so many places you could go to with a dog. Jason sometimes came along, but he had to think of his image with his mates. They laughed when they saw him going for a walk with Alison and Wolf, and made rude remarks, although they all agreed that Wolf was a beautiful dog.

. Alison couldn't avoid the kids in the street. The weather was good, dry if not always sunny, so most of them hung around in the street and saw her with Wolf. They asked questions. They stroked Wolf and offered him sweets, and sometimes asked if they could hold his lead for a while. They were the younger children.

Some of the older ones, those that Jason usually hung around with, tried to show off by teasing him. Wolf had obviously been teased before. Perhaps they used to laugh at Bobby. At the very first provocation, Wolf lunged with bared teeth and a snarl which frightened Alison as much as the rest. After that they left him alone, although one or two tried to make friends with him.

Even so, Alison would avoid them when she could. And when Jason could avoid them, too, she would find him walking along beside her, trying to be friendly while not showing too much just how much he wanted to be with Wolf.

Wolf always went wild with excitement when Jason appeared, jumping up at him, barking, getting them all muddled up in his lead. Jason didn't always stay with them. Sometimes he'd just walk along for a little way, make a fuss of Wolf, say a few abrupt words to Alison and wander off again. Sometimes he'd go with them to the park but return on his own. He couldn't seem to make up his mind about whether to stay with them or not. Sometimes he was boastful and talked too much, boring Alison stiff. Other times he was almost silent, except to talk to Wolf.

His mum had given him some money for a haircut and he was a real skinhead again, looking much tougher than Alison thought he really was. She couldn't help remembering the look on his face when he'd told her about his dog, and the way he looked when Wolf jumped all over him and soaked his face with slobbery kisses. She didn't like Jason when he was with his mates, shouting, using bad language, doing silly things like tipping over garbage cans, but mostly he was all right when he was just with her and Wolf.

Alison soon grew confident about taking Wolf out on her own. He never tried to run away from her again and, in fact, behaved himself better than a lot of dogs they met in the street. Whatever people might say about Bobby, he had certainly taught Wolf a thing or two.

Wolf was always eager to get down the stairs, and usually took little notice of Alison until they were out in the street. But she soon discovered that if she was firm enough – and that meant being really firm – Wolf would walk to heel and hardly ever pull.

When she went to the park, she didn't dare let him loose, but she bought a special nylon lead which she attached to his leather one to give him much more freedom. Often she wanted to let him go, to run about with other dogs, but she resisted the longing, unless they were out in the country. Jason showed her a place not far from the flats where she could let Wolf go. It was a big, stone-walled meadow, the playing fields of a private school. There was a painted notice saying, 'PRIVATE – TRESPASSERS WILL BE PROSECUTED', but there was never anyone there to prosecute you and, besides, Wolf didn't do any harm.

Jason said, 'Let's teach him to come when you call him. I bet he already knows, really, only you're too scared to find out.'

So Jason walked off across the playing fields with Wolf prancing along beside him and, when they were a good distance away, he let him off the lead and Alison called. Wolf shot towards her like an arrow, head low to the ground, swirling round her with the biggest of grins, delight shining in his eyes. Then Jason called, and back Wolf went again at top speed. He would do this a dozen times or more, never tiring, but once, when he found a dead magpie and nosed it about and rolled on it, he wouldn't come, however many times Alison called him. So she didn't altogether trust him.

'I bet you could teach him anything you wanted,' Jason once said. 'After all, he's a police dog, isn't he? And police dogs do all sorts of things.'

Wolf could jump the stone wall round the playing fields as easy as anything, and he could jump the gates in the farmers' fields while Alison had to climb over them. Both she and Jason tried to teach him to sit still, and not to move until he was called, but they weren't successful. Wolf just didn't want to sit still. Perhaps he sat still too long, all day in the flat. Or perhaps he just couldn't see the sense of it.

'You're not strict enough to train him properly,' Jason accused Alison, when she was fondling Wolf all over and saying how lovely he was after he'd refused to sit still.

'Well, I don't care. What difference does it make, anyway, whether he sits still or not? I just want him to have fun.'

Every evening, after she had brought him back from his walk, Alison would tie Wolf to the railings outside Mrs Bailey's flat and groom him. She hated being inside and, besides, she didn't want to do anything the way Bobby did it. She wanted Wolf to forget about Bobby.

Wolf liked being groomed. He would stand quite still, a soft look in his eyes, and only his tail would wave from side to side. In the beginning, Alison got out lots of loose hair but, bit by bit, a glow began to come to his silvery black coat, and a smoothness that made him twice as beautiful as before.

The little boys next door would watch her and sometimes give Wolf things to sniff at, no doubt feeling very brave because they dared to come so close. Their mother

75

once said, 'I hope that dog doesn't get away from you and frighten anybody. I don't think you ought to brush him out here. He's not safe.'

'He wouldn't harm a fly,' Alison defended him, and she didn't like the woman so much after that, although she'd always thought she was quite pleasant before.

Mrs Bailey would sometimes come and watch while Alison groomed Wolf, but most of the time she didn't bother. She never asked where Alison had taken him, or how Wolf behaved, and because she was always so glum Alison tried to avoid talking to her as much as possible.

When she arrived each evening Mrs Bailey would usually greet her with, 'Oh, it's you, is it? Come for Wolf?' and she'd let Alison in. Alison would say a quick 'hello', before letting Wolf overwhelm her with his greeting and, in minutes, they'd be off together, hardly noticing Mrs Bailey, who shut the door behind them.

Sometimes Mrs Bailey wasn't in and then Wolf would bark at the door, bang, scratch and whimper, but there was nothing Alison could do but talk to him and try to make him understand that it wasn't her fault. She'd go home and do her homework, then come back again, and sometimes Mrs Bailey would be home.

Mum was curious and in the end Alison had to tell her something about Wolf. She just said he was a dog she took out for an old lady who couldn't manage him herself.

'I don't know why old people keep big dogs if they can't manage them,' Mum commented, but she wasn't really interested. 'Just be careful, that's all. Don't be out too late.'

On the whole, Mum seemed quite relieved that Alison was going out more. Perhaps it gave her a greater sense of freedom. Uncle Reg came round nearly every evening. He'd offer to take them both for a drive if it was a sunny evening, but Alison always said no, impatient to be off with

Wolf. Often there would be a note from Mum, propped up on the telephone, saying, 'Out with Uncle Reg', because when Mum came in Alison had gone out, and when Alison came in, Mum had gone out. They didn't see very much of each other at all.

One day Mrs Bailey said, 'I told my Bobby about you and Wolf. He doesn't like it.'

'What do you mean?' asked Alison, suddenly gripped with fear. She couldn't stop her taking out Wolf now!

'He says Wolf's his dog and he don't want nobody else taking him out. But I told him. "Well, I can't manage him," I said, "and someone's got to exercise him." But he didn't like it. He got really upset.'

'Can't you make him understand? Can't you tell him how happy Wolf is now?'

Mrs Bailey shook her head. 'He wanted to come home with me, didn't he? To take Wolf out himself. When they wouldn't let him, he got quite nasty. He said he'll run away if they don't let him come home. He said it's my fault.'

'Do you think they will let him come home?'

Alison often wondered about Bobby coming home. She couldn't help hoping that he wouldn't. The thought was there even though she was ashamed of it. She knew she should feel sorry for Bobby, but she cared so much about Wolf that she didn't really care about Bobby at all. How could you care about somebody you didn't know?

She felt angry with Mrs Bailey for frightening her, for reminding her that Wolf belonged to someone else. Why did she tell Bobby in the first place if he was going to be angry about it?

'Can't you just pretend I don't take him out any more?' she suggested. 'He won't know, will he?'

Mrs Bailey didn't answer. She just looked grey and crushed and weary, and Alison was only too glad to get out of that miserable, airless flat, into the evening sunshine with Wolf. The very thought of Bobby depressed her.

Down in the street, she pulled Wolf close to her and hugged him tight, looking into those deeply expressive eyes of his, wondering just how much he cared about her, and whether he remembered Bobby at all, or had forgotten him.

'You're mine now,' she told him. 'One day I'm going to take you home. Oh, how I wish I could keep you for ever.'

Half-term holiday came and went, five whole weekdays without school, when Alison could be with Wolf for as long as she liked. It rained every single day, sometimes heavily, sometimes just a drizzle, but neither of them cared. Alison wore her jacket and jeans; Wolf's undercoat was thick enough to keep the rain from getting to his skin; and often they went up to the woods together, where the trees were close enough to keep the rain off, anyway.

Sometimes Alison took Wolf home, if it really was raining too much to make it sensible to go for a walk. He was restless in the flat, wanting to be out. He would pace back and forth, going to the door, whining, looking at Alison, and in the end they'd go out – just to keep him happy.

Alison showed him Goldie but Wolf, after one sniff, was as indifferent to her dream dog as he was to the Siamese cat in the hall. He was as big as the cat and made it wobble when he whacked his tail really hard against it.

'I hope you're not going to keep bringing that dog here,' Mum said to her one evening. 'There were muddy footprints everywhere when I got home. That's the trouble with dogs. Now you know why I didn't want one.'

'What's muddy footprints? You can wash them any old time,' argued Alison.

'Pity you didn't then,' said Mum sarcastically.

Mum was going away the week after half term, off to

Greece to see what kind of new hotel had been built there. For once they were having supper together. Mrs Bailey was out and Uncle Reg was away.

'It'll be lovely not to have to do anything,' Mum said, talking about her stay at the hotel. 'No bed making, no meals to cook, no washing.'

Alison didn't think Mum did much of that now, but she didn't say so, because then she'd start on about only having things to do because Alison didn't do them herself.

Mum said, 'We'll have to start thinking about that holiday with Uncle Reg, won't we?'

'I don't want to go,' replied Alison, thinking of Wolf. What would he do for two whole weeks without her?

'You're just awkward, you are,' Mum accused her, lips tightening. 'Here's poor Uncle Reg wanting to give us a good time and you don't want to know. You know how much he cares about you.'

'I didn't say *you* couldn't go. I can stay here. I'm all right on my own.'

'But he wants to take you. He wants to get to know you better. He wants you to know him.'

'I do know him already.'

Mum sighed. 'You're so awkward, aren't you? Always thinking of yourself. *I* want you to come with us.'

Alison felt tears prickling at the back of her eyes. She didn't think the accusation was fair. All she thought about was Wolf, and all Mum thought about was her job and Uncle Reg. She wanted to say this, but didn't.

'What for?' she mumbled in the end, trying to be less awkward.

Then Mum did a surprising thing. She came over to Alison and put her arms round her. She hugged her. Then she pulled up the chair beside her and sat down, putting an arm round her shoulder again.

'The thing is, Alison, Uncle Reg and I are thinking about

getting married. You'd like that, wouldn't you? I know you like him really. He's a nice man.'

Alison was so amazed she couldn't speak.

Mum hurried on. 'I know I've always said I'll never get married but . . . Well, I suppose I can change my mind. He's got a nice house over the other side of town. I've been there. It's really lovely. You'll like it. There's a big garden, and lovely views over the city. You'd have to change schools. It'd be too far to walk every day, but you'd soon settle in a new school, wouldn't you? I mean, you haven't any special friends, have you? Anyone you'd miss? And even if you did have, well, you can soon make some new friends, can't you?'

Still Alison couldn't speak. All that was in her mind was, 'What about Wolf?'

She was too stunned for anything else, too stunned even to think about Uncle Reg, and how much she'd wanted to have a dad. Just when everything was perfect, just when for the first time in her life there was some meaning to every day, something to really get up for, just when she really had something of her own . . .

'Well, say something!' Mum exclaimed. 'What are you thinking?'

'I don't want you to marry Uncle Reg. I want to stay here. I don't want you to marry him.'

Alison hardly even knew what she said. All that was in her suddenly aching heart was Wolf. Trust Mum to spoil everything! There was that feeling of panic, frightening because she couldn't control it. She jumped up from the table and ran to her room, slamming the door without realizing it, making the whole flat shake.

She threw herself down on the bed, overcome by anger, helplessness, and the unfairness of it all. Just then she hated both Mum and Uncle Reg. In her mind were all sorts of horrible things she wanted to say to them. They didn't care about her at all. They didn't ask what she wanted, what she felt. She didn't count.

She wouldn't go. Mum could go. She could go and live with Uncle Reg if she wanted, in his house, but she wasn't going. They couldn't make her. She'd stay here.

Rage and despair seethed inside her. She could almost imagine herself clinging to the doorpost as they tried to drag her out, all bags packed, other people waiting to move in. She wouldn't go. She just wouldn't go.

If only she was old enough to leave home! She'd take Wolf with her. They'd just set out one day as if they were going for a walk, and she'd get a train somewhere, or . . .

Tears rolled down her cheeks as she checked these stupid dreams. She buried her head in the pillow and sobbed. Mum didn't come in to help her.

Either nothing happens at all or, of a sudden, everything happens. Life was like that, and it didn't make sense. You could go on for ages, doing the same old things day after day, week after week, year after year – going to school, eating, sleeping, reading books, watching TV, getting bored stiff and wishing something would happen. And then, before you know what's what the world is either blossoming out in front of you, or crashing down round your ears . . .

When Alison first started to notice that dog at the window, she couldn't possibly have imagined where it was going to lead her. It had started in such a small way – that miserable, black face with hopeless eyes; that first meeting with Mrs Bailey and Wolf.

Then, bit by bit, came everything else – the walks, the grooming, a whole love relationship blossoming out of nothing, changing Alison in so many ways. Making her grow in self-confidence, making her step out into the world around her instead of escaping into the world of books, making her see people with new eyes.

All sorts of people. Not just Mrs Bailey and Jason, but people she met in the park with their dogs, and Mrs Bailey's neighbours, and the children from the flats. Through Wolf she came into some kind of relationship with all of them. She would never have imagined that through a dog you could get to know so many people.

And Wolf himself – he changed her, too, demanding so much of her, constantly putting her to the test, challenging her for mastery. There was still a lot they needed to find out about each other. Wolf, in his animal way, was still comparing her with Bobby, even comparing her with Jason, sorting them out, exploring how far he could go and what he could expect from each.

Sometimes Wolf made a complete fool of Alison, and hurt pride would make her bitterly angry. Then he would look at her with such contrition in his dark, deep eyes that anger would melt away and she would find herself hugging him instead of telling him off. Then his tail would wag and he would dance away with a kind of laughter in his eyes, having made a fool of her again. But then he would come back and lick her fingers, and they would forgive each other, and sometimes Alison thought that she was boss, and sometimes Wolf knew it was he.

Day by day they were coming to know each other better. Those days of half term, when they'd spent so many hours together ... Looking back on them, Alison could only remember how perfect they were, even though it had been wet and cold and her shoes leaked and her socks got bogged in mud.

And the evenings on the balcony together, Wolf basking in the pleasure of being groomed, of being the absolute centre of attention while enjoying all that was going on around at the same time – the little boys next door, some-one walking past him on the balcony, shouts from the street.

82

His tail wouldn't stop wagging, his big jaws were open in a constant grin.

There was something special about those hours, different from their walks together. They were only ever spoilt by Mrs Bailey when she came out to watch for a few minutes, reminding Alison just by her presence that Wolf wasn't her dog.

That was the blossoming time. Alison's life, like a plant in a pot on the shelf, had gone on in its routine, almost uneventful way, until all of a sudden flowers had budded and begun to open. Then, just when the plant was promising its best, petals bright and strong, it was as if someone had come along and knocked it off the shelf, smashing the pot, scattering the earth, breaking the stems and crushing the flowers.

Just as first seeing Wolf's face at the window had started the blossoming time, so it seemed that Mum's announcement about marrying Uncle Reg was like someone knocking down the plant pot, setting off a train of incidents that smashed up everything.

Alison's relationship with Mum had been pretty good, except over things like tidiness. They each lived their own life and were as pleasant to each other as two completely unalike people living together can be. Uncle Reg made things better, really. He had a way of drawing them together that just didn't happen when he wasn't around. And if it hadn't been for Wolf . . .

But Alison loved Wolf as she had never loved anything. Life just wouldn't be bearable without him, and she wouldn't give him up, not for anything in the world.

All her life Mum had gone on about not getting married, about being independent, about not being any man's slave – which, she told Alison, was what married life was about – and now she'd suddenly changed her tune.

All these things Alison flung at her when she could bear

to speak to her again. Mum tried to defend herself. Uncle Reg was different. He really cared about her. For the first time Mum talked about love, then went on to talk about security and a nice home and more money and things like that, so that Alison, bitter to the very depths, shouted at her, 'You don't know anything about love.'

'But what have you got against him? What difference does it make to you?' Mum asked, not understanding.

Alison couldn't bring herself to tell her. She'd never told Mum anything really important about herself, anything that really mattered – the things that hurt deep down, the things she most cared about. Gran sprang into her mind. She didn't even know why. What did Gran have to do with any of this? And yet Gran was there, somewhere, making her hurt.

If she said the name Wolf, she just knew Mum would look amazed, unbelieving. She might even laugh. She wouldn't mean to hurt her. But she wouldn't understand. And she'd make Alison give him up, just because she was Mum and, in the end, Alison always conformed to what Mum wanted. So Alison didn't have the courage to open up her heart, and perhaps have Mum bring her home an expensive china Alsatian, as near to Wolf's colouring as possible even if she had to go to ten different shops to find it.

Both of them were really relieved that, at the end of the week, Mum was going to Greece. They even managed to be nice to each other by then. Mum kept saying, 'Are you sure you'll be all right? I won't go if you don't want me to. It'll be awkward, but I can cancel it. After all, if I was ill . . .'

But Alison reassured her, and was even able to smile at her, so she went. Uncle Reg hadn't come round all week. Perhaps Mum had told him to stay away.

Alison told Jason about Uncle Reg. She had to because of the dog show that was going to be held in the park in

July. He came to tell her about it, showing her the local paper where it was mentioned. There were even entry forms to apply for.

'I know it's ages away yet, but there's these obedience classes, as well as showing classes, and I thought maybe we could teach Wolf a few things, and win a prize.'

There was a sparkle in Jason's eyes that Alison had never seen before. He was really enthusiastic. In her present mood she felt some satisfaction in crushing his eagerness.

'I don't suppose I'll even be here then, so what's the point?'

'What do you mean?' he asked.

So she told him, and he shrugged and made a gesture with his lips that suggested he knew all about the vagaries of adults anyway, and didn't expect much of them.

'Is he rotten?' he asked about Uncle Reg.

'No. He's nice.'

'Then perhaps he'll let you have Wolf if Mrs Bailey will part with him.'

'He might, but my mum wouldn't. She doesn't like dogs.'

'Then I'll look after him. He'll be all right. I'll take him out.'

That was the worst thing of all. Her misery being Jason's joy! The very thought of Wolf and Jason together, running through the fields, playing hide-and-seek in the woods, Wolf resting his big, drooling head over Jason's legs while she was stuck in a clean and tidy house miles away, with only Goldie's blank eyes to mock her, was too much to be borne.

'She might not let you,' she said.

'If you told her about me . . .'

Alison had no intention of doing that, though she didn't say so to Jason. Wolf was her dog, not Jason's, not even

85

Bobby's now. How many times had she prayed, 'Please, don't let Bobby come home? Sometimes in the middle of taking Wolf for a walk, or when she was grooming him, or when she was just sitting on the grass with him in the park, feeling full of love for him.

It was a funny kind of prayer. She didn't know if there was anyone to pray to, but it just helped her to do it, even though she knew that what she prayed was wrong. Suppose God did hear her prayer? Suppose he made it so that Bobby didn't come home? She was selfish enough to want there to be a God to make it happen, so that Wolf would be hers forever.

But after what Jason said, she was frightened. Perhaps God had heard and was going to answer her prayer, but was so angry with her for praying it that he'd let Jason have Wolf instead of her.

Even as the thought came into her head, she knew it was crazy. She wished she could talk to somebody to find out if prayers could come true. Some people said they did. Mum said it was a load of rubbish. If she said anything to Jason, he'd think she was round the bend. If Uncle Reg came round . . . Could she ask him? He always listened when she talked to him and he seemed to know a lot of things Mum didn't know.

But Uncle Reg didn't come round, and Mum went away, and Alison was in despair.

With Mum away, Alison had Wolf in the flat most of Saturday and Sunday. They didn't go out much because it rained so heavily. Wolf didn't really mind the rain. His coat was so thick that, although it might be soaked on top, if Alison pushed her fingers through his fur she found he was dry underneath. Alison didn't mind about getting wet when she was with Wolf. (She hated it on her paper round because you couldn't deliver papers with an umbrella, and they got pretty soggy at times and people complained.) But it was nice to have Wolf at home with her, stretched out on the settee, looking as if he really belonged. She could pretend that Wolf really was her dog.

She bought him a big china bowl, two big cans of meat and a box of dog biscuits, and she fed him in the kitchen. Wolf made the kitchen look quite small. When he wagged his tail it banged against the cupboards. While she was opening the tin, he put his front paws up on the counter, head cocked to one side, licking his jaws and drooling, whining because she took such a long time to open the can.

She let Wolf drink tea out of her mug. She could have put it in his bowl, but he liked it better out of the mug, and she liked it better, too. It made her laugh the way he stuck his tongue in – very carefully at first, to make sure the tea wasn't too hot. The tea splattered everywhere, all over his black muzzle as well as on the floor, and when he'd finished he licked all the drops off his muzzle and off the carpet, too, if he could find them.

On the Saturday night it was raining so heavily that Alison didn't want to take Wolf home. They were very comfortably settled on the sofa, Alison with a book, Wolf with his head stretched across her lap, not really asleep but just content to lie there with her. Now and again he nuzzled her with his nose; now and again he wriggled and made funny little sounds to draw attention to himself. He chewed her fingers or licked them, when they weren't resting on his broad head, and from time to time uttered a deep sigh of contentment.

Alison didn't feel the slightest bit lonely. She hadn't even thought about Mum in that Greek hotel. Her unhappiness couldn't last while Wolf was with her. She could push all hopeless thoughts out of her mind, and just pretend that this day with Wolf could go on and on.

Having Wolf with her all day at home made him really seem like her dog. He fitted in perfectly, as if this had always been his home. Surely he didn't remember Bobby any more? Surely, if Mum would agree, Mrs Bailey would let her keep him.

Perhaps Uncle Reg liked dogs. If he had a house with a garden, he might not mind having Wolf. Perhaps Mum marrying Uncle Reg might be a good idea after all. Alison's heart grew quite warm with excitement. If Uncle Reg said yes to Wolf, then Mum could marry him just as soon as she liked.

With Wolf keeping her warm, lying there as if he really belonged, she could believe anything and worry about nothing. And she didn't take him home that Saturday night, sure Mrs Bailey wouldn't mind, sure she'd understand – and not caring very much if she didn't.

Having Wolf spend the night there was really exciting. At first Alison thought she ought to be strict, and make him sleep in the kitchen. But there was nowhere for Wolf to sleep in the kitchen, so she left him on the sofa while she went to bed. But Wolf didn't want to be on his own.

As soon as Alison had switched off the living-room light and shut the door on him, Wolf jumped from the sofa and started barking to be let out. Alison hadn't even got into bed, and she stood in her room, wondering what to do. Wolf's barks were demanding and anxious. Should she ignore them, or go and tell him to be quiet? He began banging on the door, as he did at Mrs Bailey's, and she was scared he would scratch the paintwork. So she went back to him, pretending to be cross.

'Wolf,' she began, as she opened the door. 'You're a very naughty . . .'

He immediately jumped up and put his paws round her neck, whimpering like a baby and licking her face, so that she couldn't possibly be cross with him. Her heart melted.

'Well, all right,' she said. 'You can come to my bedroom. But you must be good and stay on the floor.'

She might have known he wouldn't. No sooner was she in bed that Wolf jumped up, nearly crushing her legs as he sprawled over the bedspread, looking very much at home.

'Oh, Wolf!' she cried, delighted even though she knew she ought not to be. 'There isn't room for both of us. This isn't your bed. It's mine.'

Wolf just stayed there, head lifted regally, his dark eyes disdainful of her protest. He had every intention of staying where he was, obviously not expecting to sleep anywhere else.

Alison dragged her legs free and managed to squeeze herself into a half-comfortable position. She couldn't read, too much aware of Wolf's eyes constantly on her face. In the end she switched off the lamp, pushed him hard with her foot to make him move over just a bit, and soon felt him wriggling himself up closer to her so that her outstretched arm could comfortably lie across his shoulders. Like that, they both fell asleep.

Sunday was just as good. Alison felt so cheerful that she even cooked herself a proper meal and made enough to share with Wolf. He sat close to her while she ate, ears pricked, jaws dripping, and she kept giving him chips and bits of hamburger. He licked up the dirty plate afterwards – even the ketchup – and made it look as though it didn't need washing, and he had no trouble getting his tongue into the plastic trifle cup for the bits of jelly and custard she'd left there for him.

They went for a long walk in the afternoon, in spite of the rain. There was hardly a soul in the park, so Alison let him off the lead for once and watched him race across the sloping lawns, quite sure that he would return to her.

When they went back, they had tea and toast, and some

fruit cake, and Alison's heart began to sink as she thought about taking Wolf home. She didn't want to take him back to Mrs Bailey ever again, but it was school tomorrow and she dared not leave him all day in the flat on his own.

Mrs Bailey was pretty nasty to her when Alison went back with Wolf. Right on the doorstep, she started to tell her off.

'You had me that worried,' she said. 'I thought something had happened, didn't I? That Wolf was in trouble and you didn't dare come and tell me. You shouldn't have done it. I haven't slept all night, wondering. And then all day today. No sign of you. That's the trouble with you young people today. Got no thought for other people.'

'I'm sorry, Mrs Bailey, really I am,' exclaimed Alison, though in her heart she wasn't, she'd enjoyed herself so much. Just then she felt like taking Wolf home again with her and never coming back. Instead she forced herself to promise, 'I won't do it again.'

'No, you'd better not. My Bobby doesn't like you having him out, anyway. He doesn't understand, but I don't want to upset him. He gets ever so upset he does, and he only wants to talk about Wolf when I go to see him. I was there this afternoon. Just got back.'

Her face seemed to crumple as she spoke, as if that effort at anger had been too much for her. For a moment her eyes met Alison's, but Alison quickly escaped the look, embarrassed by it. She knew she ought to ask Mrs Bailey about Bobby, but she didn't want to hear. She wanted to forget that Bobby even existed. All she cared about was Wolf and she was scared Bobby might persuade Mrs Bailey not to let her take him out.

'I've got to go,' she cried. 'I'll be back tomorrow. Goodbye, Wolf.'

She knelt down and hugged him tight. Wolf licked her face and made to go with her as she went to the door. He didn't want to stay behind. It really hurt Alison to have to tell him he couldn't come. He put his head on one side and listened without understanding.

In the end, she had to take him back to Bobby's room and shut the door to keep him from following her. He yelped and banged and barked, and waited expectantly. Alison's heart ached as she went away, hearing Mrs Bailey's weary voice shouting for him to shut up.

With the weekend over, the sun returned, beating on the school window panes, its glaring heat making lessons even harder to concentrate on than usual. All the windows were wide open and now and again a wasp would sweep in, refusing to leave until it had cowed most of the girls in the classroom. But at least it woke them up.

Alison wondered what poor Wolf was doing in this heat. He panted enough when he was outdoors. So what would it be like for him, shut up in the flat? She remembered the first time she had gone there, how suffocating and smelly it was, and her heart went out to Wolf. She promised herself that she'd take him for a really long walk that evening, to his favourite place – the woods. And though her eyes were open, staring at the blackboard where Mr Giles laboured over an algebraic equation for her benefit, her mind was far away.

She was at Mrs Bailey's just after four o'clock, hardly giving herself time to change out of her uniform. Wolf was locked up in Bobby's room. She could hear him bark and clamour in reply to the bell as Mrs Bailey shuffled to the door. There was a darkness about her expression that Alison hadn't seen before. Her eyes were swollen as if she'd been crying, though they weren't red.

'I don't want you coming round here no more,' were her first words. 'That dog's been driving me round the bend all day and night. He was all right till you came along. You've changed him. You've ruined him, and I can't stand no more of it, see.'

'But what's the matter? What have I done?' cried Alison, bewildered, hardly able to believe this was happening.

Mrs Bailey's eyes looked haunted.

'He's done nothing but whine, whine, whine, and bark, bark, bark. I've had the neighbours banging on the walls. They've threatened to call the police. I just don't know what to do.'

Wolf was going crazy behind the bedroom door. He had heard Alison's voice and was desperate to get out.

'Please let me see him.' she cried. 'Please. Just listen to him. He – '

'I've done nothing but listen to him. I can't keep him quiet. Up and down all day he's been, trying to get out. I daren't even open the door. What with him and Bobby, they'll be the death of me. I just can't cope any more. I've had enough.'

'Please let me take him out, Mrs Bailey. He'll be all right if I take him out. I know he will. He only wants his walk.'

'And when he comes back? What then? He'll be whining again, wanting to be with you. No. No. I've had enough. Go away. Leave us alone,' and she slammed the door in Alison's face.

It seemed to slam right through Alison's brain. She just stood there, unable to think, unable to move. It couldn't all be finished, just like that – not after that wonderful weekend, not when she and Wolf were really belonging to each other at last. It just didn't make sense.

Wolf was still barking. Mrs Bailey was silent. Perhaps she'd given up trying to quieten him and was just leaving him in Bobby's room, trying to forget he was there. Alison couldn't bear it.

She rang the bell again, several times, determined to

make Mrs Bailey see sense. She'd tell her that she would have Wolf. She could keep him till Mum came home, and worry about what might happen afterwards. Maybe Mum would understand. She'd tell Mum she could marry Uncle Reg if only she'd let her keep Wolf. Surely Mum would say yes. Surely Mrs Bailey would say yes. Everything was so simple, really. It was grown-ups that made life so complicated.

Angry, impatient, despairing, Alison rang the bell not caring what promises she made that couldn't be kept, so long as she could get Wolf out of that room. But Mrs Bailey wouldn't answer, and Wolf went on barking and barking.

The woman next door came out on to the balcony, looking at Alison with thunder in her eyes.

'I'll have that dog put down, I will,' she cried. 'We can't sleep at night. It wakes up the kids. She's no right to keep it like that.'

'What do you know about it?' shouted back Alison. 'It's not his fault.'

'I don't care whose fault it is. It's a scandal, that's what I say. I pay my rent and I've got my rights. I'm not putting up with any more of it.'

She started ringing Mrs Bailey's bell, too, and banging on the door. 'I'll have the police round,' she shouted, furious because Mrs Bailey wouldn't open up.

Alison stood back, watching her in horror. There was something frightening about adults when they lost control of themselves, and she ran off, feeling sick with fear.

Back home, she tried to do her homework, but couldn't concentrate. She couldn't eat and even the cup of coffee she'd made for herself tasted like sawdust. She decided to walk round the block and look up at Wolf's window, to see if he was there. At least she could see him, if nothing else. If only he would notice her, too! But Wolf wasn't at the window. Surely he wasn't still barking at the bedroom door?

A frightening thought hit her. Suppose the police had come and taken him away? Her heart beat so fast that she went all dizzy. Would they come so quickly?

Almost against her own will, afraid of what she might discover, Alison returned to Mrs Bailey's flat. There was no one about. She stood outside the door, listening. Silence! Wolf had either shut up at last, or he'd been taken away.

Dare she ring the bell? No, she didn't. If he was quiet she didn't want to disturb him. If he'd been taken away . . .

Shaken, confused, she went down the stairs again and looked for Jason. Just then she needed someone to talk to. But he was nowhere around and she didn't know where he lived. She wouldn't have gone to his flat, anyway. From what he said, his mother sounded like an awful woman.

She went home and waited and waited for Uncle Reg to come. Mum said he'd pop in to see her while she was away. But he didn't. Perhaps he didn't like her any more. Eventually, she went to bed. She couldn't sleep, remembering how Wolf had been with her such a short while ago. Was it all just a dream, turned into a nightmare, or had it really happened? For the first time she wished Mum was home, so she could talk to her and cry. She longed so much to cry, but tears just wouldn't come.

Next morning, when she did her paper round, Alison's heart leapt with joy because Wolf was at the window. He was still at home. He hadn't been taken away. But his eyes had that blank stare she always used to see, and which had disappeared over the last few weeks. Now it was back.

Alison's throat was choked as she stared up at him. What must he think of her? How could he understand? She willed him to look down at her, but he didn't. He just stared ahead at nothing, as he always used to.

School went on for ever. As soon as she was let free Alison hurried round to Mrs Bailey's. She was determined

94

to talk to her, prepared to tell her any amount of lies as long as she could persuade Mrs Bailey to let her take Wolf out, or at least come in to see him.

Perhaps Mrs Bailey wouldn't be so upset today. Perhaps yesterday was just a bad day, what with the neighbours being so mean. Alison couldn't bring herself to believe that Wolf wouldn't be there, that he might have been taken away while she was at school.

She had to pass a greengrocer's on the way. There were some pink and white carnations outside, so Alison thought she'd take some to Bobby's gran to cheer her up. Perhaps she liked flowers, and she couldn't not let her in if she'd brought her a present. Alison bought half a dozen. The assistant put them in a piece of fancy paper with a stalk of feathery green, and they looked quite pretty. Surely Mrs Bailey would be pleased?

Wolf wasn't at the window, and again the pain and fear that was becoming familiar attacked Alison. She raced up the stairs and rang Mrs Bailey's bell urgently, several times. Relief swept over her as she heard Wolf's voice. She felt like laughing and crying at the same time. But he was in Bobby's room, so she couldn't talk to him.

Mrs Bailey didn't come to the door. Was she out? Or did she just guess it was Alison and refuse to answer.

'Oh please, please let me in,' Alison begged under her breath, clutching the carnations. But there was no sound, except Wolf's barking.

Alison decided to return after tea. Perhaps Mrs Bailey had gone shopping, or to see Bobby. When she came the second time she forgot to bring the flowers, but it didn't matter because again Mrs Bailey seemed to be out. Wolf barked frantically. The neighbour's television was blaring so loudly that Alison could hear every word. Perhaps she had put it loud on purpose to annoy Mrs Bailey, because of Wolf.

Alison went home and did her homework. Then she came back. It was half past eight. Still Mrs Bailey didn't answer the door. Poor Wolf just barked and barked, and Alison stood outside in despair, listening to him.

Wolf wasn't at the window next morning. Had the police come at last? Had he been taken away? Alison was very much tempted to run up to Mrs Bailey's flat there and then to find out. But it was so early, not even eight o'clock. If Mrs Bailey was still in bed it wouldn't put her in a very good mood. No, she'd have to wait till after school. Somehow she would have to bear with the suspense till then.

School that day went on even longer than the day before. Every minute was like an hour. Inside, Alison felt sick the whole time, as if she knew something dreadful had happened, or was going to happen. She kept telling herself it was nonsense. How many times had she thought Wolf had been taken away, only to discover he was still there? The neighbours shouted and complained but they didn't actually do anything.

On the way home she kept repeating under her breath, 'Please let Mrs Bailey be home. Please let Wolf be there. Please let me take him out.'

It was like a magic formula. If she kept on saying it, everything would be all right – except she knew it wasn't true. Things didn't happen just because you wanted them to.

The hope and dread in her heart were almost too painful to bear as she came past Wolf's window on the other side of the road, and looked up. He wasn't there!

But that doesn't mean anything, she told herself insistently, though she had to bite her lips to keep back the tears prickling in her eyes. She'd go home and get the flowers and then she'd know. Only a short while more . . .

As she came up the hill she saw Jason. She had avoided

him all weekend, not wanting to share Wolf with him, and this was the first time she'd seen him in days.

'You heard about Mrs Bailey?' he greeted her, his eyes alight with a strange kind of excitement.

'No. What's happened?' Alison felt herself going dizzy with fear.

'She's done herself in, hasn't she?'

'You what?'

'Took an overdose. They carted her off in an ambulance this morning. A boy at school told me. He lives upstairs from her and he was off school this morning. Went to the dentist, or something. Anyway, when he came back there was all this racket, see. Police, ambulance, the lot. You know. And his mum went down to find out. They had to break the door down.'

'What for?' Alison couldn't take it in.

"Cause of Wolf. He was making this horrible racket, see. Whining and everything. Wouldn't stop. And the neighbours thought it was suspicious. So they called the police, 'cause she wouldn't open the door.'

'You're making it up,' Alison accused him. 'You're really rotten, Jason Harding. It's just the sort of thing you would think of.'

'I'm not,' he cried. 'It's all true. Honest. If you don't believe me, go and find out for yourself. They've bust the door. They've put a padlock on it. Go on. I'll come with you if you like.'

Dazed, unwilling, Alison followed Jason up the stairs. As soon as she reached the balcony she knew he wasn't lying because of the neighbour who was standing out there. She could tell by the look on her face. She stared hard at Alison for a moment, then went back into her own flat and slammed the door.

Alison couldn't take another step. It was a hot afternoon but she felt as if iced water had suddenly been poured down her spine. She could feel the sun on her face even as she turned to ice inside. Her mind was a blank. Only her heart still functioned, swelling to unbearable proportions, though she didn't even know what was hurting so much inside her.

She saw Jason staring at her, and his face seemed weird and unrecognizable. He looked as though he didn't care one bit, except for the excitement that it gave to the day. That grin of his . . . And his eyes screwed up against the sun. Was he mocking, or was he just as helpless as she was in the face of something neither of them could understand?

'What about Wolf?' she said.

If he answered, she didn't hear him or it didn't register. She went home. Jason walked with her. Neither of them said anything, and she didn't invite him in. She threw down her bag by the Siamese cat, then sat at the kitchen table. The sun blazed in through the window, as if it were a lovely day.

Alison's mind started to function again, only she wished it hadn't because all she could think about was Mrs Bailey. She always looked as if she wanted something you couldn't give her, something you ought to be able to give her, even though you didn't know what it was. That look had always been there, and it had made Alison feel uncomfortable. She knew she had always rather despised Mrs Bailey. She was so drab, so hopeless, so . . . Her every word was a moan or a sigh. People like that got you down. It wasn't Alison's fault if she couldn't like her. And yet . . .

As she sat at the small table, staring at the clean kitchen walls bright with sunlight, Alison suddenly understood that Mrs Bailey had been as lonely and as desperate as Wolf; as much a prisoner as he was, staring out speechlessly at an uncaring world, no longer expecting anything good.

But Wolf had a beautiful face. And he was a dog. It was

easy to love a dog. They asked so little of you. They looked at you with love and never expected more than you could give them. Dogs gave you so much in exchange for so little. Just the way Wolf looked at her, the way he opened his big jaws and cocked his head, pricked his ears and wagged his tail . . . You couldn't help loving him and wanting to do things for him.

If it hadn't been for Wolf, Alison would never have known Mrs Bailey, never have talked to her, never have found out about Bobby. And yet, what did she know about her? Almost nothing. Would anyone tell Bobby what had happened to her? Was there anyone left to care about him?

It was all too much for Alison. Guilt, shame, bewilderment flooded her with confused anguish. She couldn't even say sorry. It was too late. Her eyes caught the carnations, wilting in the sun on the draining board where she had left them yesterday. Even that little gift hadn't been a genuine one. And then she wept.

Some time later the doorbell rang. Alison didn't want to answer. Her head ached and her eyes were swollen. It might be Jason, and what was there to say to him? It rang again, more insistently, and the sharp but silly hope came to her that it might be someone with news about Wolf – or Jason telling her that Mrs Bailey wasn't dead after all, that they'd saved her life at the last minute in hospital.

'Who's there?' she called through the door.

'It's me, Sunshine. Aren't you going to let me in?'

Uncle Reg!

For a moment Alison hesitated. Only the night before she'd wanted him badly and he hadn't come. Now . . . She tried to remember why she had wanted him, but her poor head was too tired and aching to sort it out. He called again and automatically she opened the door, unable to look at him because already tears were beginning to choke her again.

'What's all this? What's all this?' he exclaimed in a jocular manner that quickly became serious when she just stood there, letting the tears pour unchecked down her face.

'Here!' he exclaimed. 'You're really upset about something, aren't you? You'd better tell me all about it.'

It wasn't so much the words, but the way he said them – as if he really cared, really wanted to comfort her – that took Alison right into the arms he folded round her. She pressed her wet face and runny nose against his jacket, and just gave herself up to him until the weeping was truly spent. He didn't ask anything. He just held her close and stroked her head and said a few gentle words, and after a while she felt strangely comforted and didn't want to cry any more.

Uncle Reg let her go, smiling at her in a way that made her smile back.

'That's better,' he said. 'Perhaps now you can tell me what it's all about, what's happened.'

She told him in a muddled way about Mrs Bailey, and Bobby, and Wolf, and when she'd finished he asked, 'And what are you crying about? Everything, or just Wolf?'

'Everything,' she confessed humbly, 'because everything is so horrible. The neighbours, me, Bobby being taken away when he didn't really do anything bad, and nobody caring about Mrs Bailey. I only cared about Wolf.'

'It's easier to care about a dog,' said Uncle Reg, as if he knew what she herself had been thinking.

'But I should have cared about Mrs Bailey, too.'

'Yes, I suppose you should. But it wasn't just you. It was everybody. Bobby's mum, for example. Where's she? Everybody's selfish, you see. We only think about what *we* want. We don't care about anybody else. We leave society to look after other people. Only society is us, so we're back to square one.'

'What can I do?' she begged.

'About Mrs Bailey? Nothing. It's too late to do anything for her, isn't it?'

'It's so awful,' she cried.

'Yes,' he agreed. His face looked sad, and at least he didn't tell her not to worry, as Mum would have done. He didn't tell her it was none of her business, and not to get involved. He looked as though he cared about Mrs Bailey even though he didn't know her.

'I kept praying Bobby wouldn't come home, so I could keep Wolf,' she confessed.

'That wasn't a nice thing to do, was it?'

She shook her head. 'And now Bobby won't ever be allowed home because he hasn't got a home to go to any more. And I expect it's my fault.'

Uncle Reg looked thoughtful. 'Not your fault,' he said at last, 'but it's bound to make you feel guilty because you know it was a wrong thing to do.'

'Do you think if I prayed again things would be different?' she begged hopefully.

He shook his head. 'You can't change what's happened. All you can do now is try to sort things out to carry on from where you are.'

She asked him if he thought God really existed and he said, 'If he didn't, then everything would be senseless.'

It was a comforting answer, even though it added to her shame, and at last, while Uncle Reg made a cup of tea for them both and had his back to her for a minute, Alison was able to bring up the worry that was closest to her heart.

'And what about Wolf?'

Uncle Reg turned to give her a look that told her he already knew what she was going to ask next.

'I think the best thing would be for me to get in touch

with the police and find out what's happening all round –
about Bobby, and Wolf, and everything.'

'Oh, Uncle Reg, would you really?'

Alison put her arms round him and hugged him as hard
as she could. Suddenly she knew she loved him and wanted
more than anything for him to be her Dad. But she was too
shy to say so with words. Somehow she felt he understood.
He gave her a special kind of grin, then went to the
phone.

'You just keep that tea hot,' he said. 'I can't stand cold
tea.'

The police didn't tell Uncle Reg a lot but he did find out
where Wolf was – at the S.P.C.A. kennels about three miles
away. Uncle Reg phoned them up but there was only a
recorded voice telling him to leave a message or ring the
next morning.

'Did you tell them about Wolf, that he belongs to me?'
cried Alison anxiously.

'No. I didn't say anything. I can't stand those answering
machines. I'm a human being, I am. I'm not talking to a
flipping machine.'

'But suppose . . .'

'Not to worry,' he comforted her. 'I'll ring them up from
work tomorrow and make arrangements for us to go and
see him. Would you like that?'

She nodded fiercely, unable to speak, still anxious and
almost angry with Uncle Reg because, like a typical adult,
he seemed to think she could easily wait for tomorrow and
just go on living as if nothing could happen between now
and then. Tomorrow was a lifetime away. And how could
Wolf understand what tomorrow was all about?

Uncle Reg broke in on her speechlessness. 'And what are
we going to do about him?' he said.

Alison met his eyes for a moment then looked away, hardly

daring to say all that she wanted to say. If she'd expected in that quick moment to see a solution on Uncle Reg's face, she was disappointed. He wasn't just teasing. It was a genuine question. Surely he must know what was in her heart? And, if so, why did he ask?

'Your mum doesn't like dogs, does she?' he went on.

'She says they're messy.'

'She'd never change her mind about a dog like Wolf. I shouldn't think he's quite her style, would you?'

'Mum only likes china dogs,' was Alison's bitter reply.

Uncle Reg poured himself a cup of tea, put in two large spoonfuls of sugar, and stirred thoughtfully.

'It's a bit of a problem, isn't it?' he said. 'I mean, if we do go to see him, he'll probably expect you to bring him home, won't he?'

'Oh, Uncle Reg, will you let me? Mum's still away. If Wolf's here when she gets back she can't turn him out, can she? She can't just chuck him out in the street. She'll have to put up with him. Oh, Uncle Reg, let's go and get him tomorrow. Let's bring him home quick.'

'Hey, steady on now. Steady on. 'Course I want to help you, if I can, but we've got to be sensible about these things. How do you think your mum would feel, coming back from Greece all tired and sunburnt, wanting to put her feet up from the long journey, and finding a great big dog jumping about all over the place. And then you telling her it was me that brought him home?'

'It wouldn't matter. She'd be mad at first, but she'd get over it.'

'Oh, would she? You say that because you're only thinking of yourself. Just imagine what I'd come in for? A flipping great rollicking. She might never speak to me again.'

Alison didn't know if Uncle Reg was talking seriously or not. He looked serious and yet there was always a kind of

103

smile about him, as if everything was half a joke.

'Still,' he went on, 'I don't suppose that'd bother you too much.'

'What?'

'Your mum not speaking to me again. I don't think you'd care about anything, as long as you got what you wanted.'

Alison felt the recrimination in his tone and snapped back resentfully, 'It's what everybody else does, isn't it – get what they want? Why shouldn't I?'

Uncle Reg didn't have an answer. He sipped his tea and looked at the dead flowers on the draining board. 'Who were they for?' he said.

'Mrs Bailey. I forgot to take them to her.'

There was an uncomfortable silence between them. Alison again felt that everything had gone wrong. Uncle Reg seemed to be expecting something of her. She knew that what she had just said sounded awful, about getting what she wanted like everyone else, but at least it was true. So why pretend otherwise?

Uncle Reg sighed and then said, 'Look, Sunshine, just try to imagine how your mum would feel if she saw a hulking great dog here. She might send it back to the S.P.C.A., and then where would you be?'

Alison pulled a face, desperately unhappy inside. Just a short while ago – before Uncle Reg poured himself the tea – things seemed to be going all right. Now, even before he'd finished drinking it, everything was going wrong again. He wasn't on her side at all. No one would be on her side. No one cared about Wolf, except maybe Jason.

A new tear slid down her cheek. Her lips trembled.

'You can't put your mum in that situation,' Uncle Reg tried to explain. 'It's not fair to her. You'd hate her if she sent Wolf away again, wouldn't you?'

'Then what can I do?' Alison almost squeaked, trying so hard not to cry.

'You'll have to try and get round her, won't you,' he said. 'You're a very determined young lady when it suits you.'

'She'll never say yes.'

'You can't blame her, not in a flat like this. I expect it's against the rules, anyway, keeping dogs. You wouldn't want your mum to have all the trouble with the neighbours that poor old Mrs What's-her-name had, would you?'

'People are horrible.'

'Well, you're "people" too,' said Uncle Reg.

Alison had no answer to that.

There was silence while Uncle Reg poured himself a second cup of tea. He really seemed to be expecting Alison to say something, but she didn't know what it was. He'd go in a minute, and Alison didn't want him to go, afraid of being alone, sure she'd never get through tonight and tomorrow, waiting to know about Wolf.

She could ask him to stay a bit longer, but she was still angry with him because somehow it seemed that he was angry with her. Why did he say not to worry, as if everything would be all right, and then as good as tell her that she'd probably never be able to have Wolf?

'I thought you cared,' she accused him at last, her voice low, filled with misery, but her heart hardening even as she spoke.

'I care about your mum,' he said. 'I want to marry her. I care about you, quite a bit.'

'Then why won't you let me have Wolf?'

'I haven't said you can't have him. I just said you can't bring him home here while your mum's away and expect her to accept him, just like that.'

A sharp hope sprang to Alison's heart.

'You've got a garden, haven't you, Uncle Reg? If Mum said yes, we could have him at your house, couldn't we? He wouldn't be in the way if we had a garden.'

'We?' said Uncle Reg, looking at her hard.

Alison found her face going red. Uncomfortably, she forced herself to go on with her new idea.

'Well, if you and Mum get married, then we could have Wolf at your house, couldn't we? I mean, you wouldn't mind, would you? You could have Mum, and I could have Wolf.'

'Thanks very much,' said Uncle Reg.

He sounded quite sarcastic but Alison rushed on, 'It'd be all right. I'd pay for his food and everything, and I wouldn't let him be a nuisance.'

'Your mum told me you were dead against us getting married so . . .'

'I don't care,' Alison interrupted hotly, 'so long as I can have Wolf.'

'Well, I expect you'll get him, one way or another,' said Uncle Reg, getting up from the kitchen table. 'As I said, you're a very determined young lady. Anyway, I must be off. I'll let you know tomorrow what they tell me about Wolf at the S.P.C.A.'

He was making for the door and Alison felt desperately unhappy. She didn't want him to go, but she didn't know how to make him stay. Her heart was in turmoil. She wanted to cry, 'Please don't go,' but she was angry, too, because he didn't care as much as she did.

'Bye,' she said to him at the door, not meeting his eyes.

'Bye,' he replied, hesitating a moment. 'You'll be all right,' he added, with a last effort at comfort, and then he walked away.

Alison watched him, wishing he'd turn round and come back. So many things surged in her heart. She wanted to tell him that she loved him, that she really wanted him to be her dad. But she didn't know how to. It was too embarrassing, too painful.

Now she knew that she'd done it all wrong, that she'd

upset Uncle Reg by saying she didn't care. She didn't really mean that she didn't care. She just didn't know how to put it. Oh, why did people always take words so seriously? Why was it so easy to say the wrong thing and hurt people so badly, when you didn't really want to hurt them at all?

There was still time to call out, 'Uncle Reg!' He'd come back. She knew he would. But then, how would she tell him? How would she explain? How would she say, 'I want you to be my dad'?

She could talk about loving Wolf. That was easy. It was loving people that was so hard to confess. She'd go all red and not know what to say. And again she felt angry with him – and with Mum. He should have already been her dad, right from the beginning, and then she wouldn't have had to say anything.

Even as she thought these things Uncle Reg turned to go down the stairs. He looked back and waved cheerfully, and she lifted her hand to wave back. Then he was gone, and it was too late.

Uncle Reg did telephone the S.P.C.A. the next day but he was too busy to come round in the evening to see Alison. He was an insurance agent and sometimes he had to see clients in the evening.

'Are you sure you're all right?' he asked Alison over the phone. She nodded, and then remembered to say yes, glad that he couldn't see the tears that sprang to her eyes.

'Look,' he said. 'It'll soon be the weekend, and your mum will be back from Greece. We'll take her to see Wolf. How about that?'

He sounded eager to cheer her up, eager to please.

'The police told me they keep dogs for ever at that place. Not like some. Some places they put them down after a few days, but at our S.P.C.A. they keep them till they die of old age, so there's no worry about anything happening to Wolf, is there? 'He'll still be there on Sunday.'

'But if Mum won't let me have him?'

'Don't worry, Sunshine. Let's cross our bridges when we come to them. Okay?'

She said okay, but she didn't feel okay. There were still two nights and a whole day before Mum came home, and she wouldn't want to go and see him the same day. Suppose the kennels didn't open on Sundays? What then? It was much easier to despair than to hope.

Alison had no reason to hope that Mum would care at all, and there was a distance between herself and Uncle Reg that hadn't been there before. She knew it was her fault, not his, but she didn't know how to overcome it.

Even so, her greatest anxiety was for Wolf. What was he doing? How could he understand what had happened to him? Did he long for her? Did he miss Mrs Bailey and his old home? Had he loved Bobby's gran, even if only a little bit? Everything had gone wrong in Wolf's life, too.

Did dogs have hopes and fears like humans do? Alison didn't know, but she suffered for Wolf because there was nothing within her power that she could do for him.

For a while she thought about going on her own to the kennels. She saw Jason and talked about it with him, hoping he might go with her. But Jason only made her feel worse.

'Waste of time,' he said. 'They won't take no notice of you. You're only a kid. What can you do? They might not even let you see him.'

'But we could try,' she pleaded, needing his support.

'Huh! It won't get you nowhere. They let you say everything, but they don't take no notice. And, anyway, Wolf bit one of them policemen that came to the flat. He had to go to hospital. I bet they'll have him put down.'

Jason seemed to be getting some kind of satisfaction out of all this. Alison couldn't understand him, but she knew he wouldn't help her.

'I thought you cared about Wolf,' she accused him angrily.

'Me? I don't care about nothing. What's the point? When you care about something, you only lose it.'

'You do if you don't care. I care about Wolf, and I'm not going to lose him. It's when you don't care that things happen.'

'Oh yeah?' he sneered. 'If you get Wolf back, maybe I'll believe you. But I haven't got nothing back yet. I bet old Mrs Bailey cared about Bobby, didn't she? Did she get him back?'

Alison was shocked into silence by his bitterness. There was nothing she could say and, as he went off up the hill, swaggering and kicking at an empty grocery box that was lying on the pavement, she couldn't help feeling that Jason had already put both Wolf and herself out of his life altogether.

She went home and stood in the hall. It was only a small hall. The Siamese cat took up most of the room, and just then he looked so cold and smug and above everything that mattered that Alison could almost have smashed his head off, just to let out of herself the things that were bursting inside.

But she wasn't the kind of person that smashed things – not like Jason – and eventually she just went to her room and sat on her bed. She couldn't even cry.

She remembered what Jason had said, and the look on his face, almost a look of triumph because what he believed about the world was coming true in Alison's life, too. It had been true for Mrs Bailey. Bobby had been taken away from her. Maybe he was a bit funny, maybe he didn't fit in any-where. She loved him, but she didn't know how to help him and nobody cared.

It was a bitter time for Alison, trying to square up in her heart and mind what life should be like, and what it really was. So many thoughts came and went – people, too, like

109

Gran, who lived on her own and hardly ever saw her family; and Uncle Reg who had loved his wife, who died, and now wanted to marry Mum. And Mum herself who, until now at least, had never wanted to care about anyone for very long. Maybe she was scared of losing what she loved, too.

Alison tried to imagine not loving Wolf. After all, until a short while ago she hadn't even known that he existed. She'd lived without him before. But that *was* before. Afterwards was different.

She felt she would really hate Mum and Uncle Reg if she couldn't have Wolf, and for a little while she raged inside with resentment towards them both. But she couldn't keep it up. First of all, it hurt too much, and secondly she knew Uncle Reg really cared about her. She supposed Mum did, too, only she wasn't very good at saying so. Uncle Reg showed it in lots of ways, and sort of said it, too.

Then her heart ached again, in a new way, because she did want Uncle Reg to marry Mum; because she wanted him to belong to her, too. She didn't want him to go away. She really, really wanted him to be her dad, and she could hardly wait for Mum to come home so she could tell her. It would be easy to tell Mum. Alison was used to hiding her feelings from Mum. She would just casually mention it as soon as she got off the plane.

So a little bit of hope did creep in as she longed and longed for Mum to be home, just so that she could tell her about Uncle Reg. There wasn't any thought of Wolf in that hope. Wolf was now a separate issue. Whether she got him back or not, she still wanted Mum and Uncle Reg to get married.

When eventually she went to bed and put out the light, head aching, heart weary, her thoughts somehow turned to that mysterious God who Uncle Reg said was real. And she said to him, 'I'm sorry for all the horrid things I prayed about Bobby.'

She couldn't help remembering how she'd prayed for him not to come home and she felt ashamed. She couldn't say more than that about him, but her heart hurt so much that surely God would know. Then she said, 'You know what it's all about. Please sort it all out for me.'

Jason came into her mind. 'And help Jason, too.'

She didn't say much, but somehow it seemed to help. Her head stopped aching and there was peace in her heart. She fell asleep.

Saturday came at last. Alison went with Uncle Reg to the airport to collect Mum. She wasn't anxious about Wolf now, sure that Uncle Reg would sort everything out. In the car, he told her to leave things to him, and not to worry about Mum because he knew how to get round her.

Alison didn't say much at all. Unexpectedly, she felt strangely shy with Uncle Reg, as if already they had a different relationship – a much closer one which needed to be very cautiously expanded.

Alison's main desire as they waited for the charter plane to land and come to a standstill and disembark its passengers was to tell Mum she'd changed her mind about Uncle Reg. She was so busy thinking about it, and getting impatient because everything took so long, that she forgot all about Uncle Reg standing silently beside her.

When at last Mum came through the barrier – looking sunburnt and weary as Uncle Reg had promised she would – before Alison could go forward to meet her, Uncle Reg was already there. His arms were round her, in spite of her suitcase and bulging plastic bags, and he gave her such a long kiss that Alison didn't know how she could breathe. She suddenly realized that Uncle Reg had missed Mum more than she had.

Uncle Reg took all the bits and pieces and led the way to the car. Mum said to Alison, 'How've you been?' Alison said, 'Gosh, I do hope you and Uncle Reg are going to get married soon,' and Mum shot her such a surprised and grateful look that Alison, for once, felt all good inside. Perhaps Mum did need someone to look after her, only she hadn't found the right person before.

On Sunday they went to the S.P.C.A. kennels. Mum had heard all about Wolf and Mrs Bailey, and she wasn't too happy. Uncle Reg had somehow convinced her that she ought to go and see Wolf before making up her mind about him, but she kept on saying, 'Alsatians are such big dogs. I don't like them. Why can't she have a little dog, if she must have a dog?'

'She doesn't want a little dog,' Uncle Reg patiently explained, 'she wants Wolf.' And when Mum wasn't looking he gave Alison a wink to remind her not to worry, and to keep her mouth shut till the time was right.

It was a rainy day. The kennels were at the bottom of a rough lane, in the middle of a field. There was mud everywhere, which Mum didn't like. Her high-heeled shoes kept getting stuck in it. She held on to Uncle Reg's arm and grumbled about the weather, going on about how hot and sunny it was in Greece and why did anybody bother to live in England? And what a silly way to spend a Sunday, going to a dogs' home!

They had to go to the office first. There were several people there, looking for dogs, and some who turned out to be volunteer dog-walkers. Alison was feeling dreadfully nervous again. Mum wasn't convinced one little bit about having ing Wolf when she and Uncle Reg were married, which was what Uncle Reg had suggested – much to Alison's delight – and Alison wanted Mum to see him this first time looking beautiful and proud.

She wondered if the kennel girls groomed him, or if he would let them. She wondered if he would be out in the rain, or have a nice, cosy kennel to shelter in. She herself was nervous of seeing him again. It seemed a lifetime since their weekend together, which at this point was more a remembered dream than something that had actually happened.

At this point, too, it all seemed too good to be true. Uncle Reg actually wanting Wolf, Mum thinking about it, all of them about to see him just as soon as the formalities were got through.

Uncle Reg did the talking, reminding the man at the desk how he had rung up about Wolf a few days earlier. The man had a big book which registered all the dogs in the kennels and when they had been brought in.

He looked up the date, his finger found Wolf's description. There was some writing in the widest column at the end, which he looked through carefully a couple of times before saying to Uncle Reg, 'Can you wait here a minute, please?' and getting up to go and talk to someone in another room. A few minutes later he returned with a woman who looked at Alison and then at Mum and then at Uncle Reg.

'These are the people,' the man said to her.

At his words Alison's heart seemed to turn over and sink. She just knew that something was wrong.

'This dog,' began the woman, pausing to look at Uncle Reg. 'He doesn't actually belong to you, does he?'

'No, but . . .' and Uncle Reg went on to explain just how they knew about Wolf.

The woman listened politely and then said, 'You see, when he was brought here from the police station we were told he was quite a dangerous dog. He's bitten several people, including two policemen.'

'He doesn't like policemen,' broke in Alison. 'And it wasn't his fault. He was only defending Bobby and . . .'

'You never told me he bites!' exclaimed Mum. 'I don't want anything to do with a dog that bites.'

'He wouldn't bite me. He's never bitten me. He loves

113

me. I bet he only bit that policeman the other day because of what happened. He probably thought they were hurting Mrs Bailey. He – '

Uncle Reg interrupted her, putting a hand on her shoulder. 'Hang on a minute,' he said. 'We won't get anything sorted out if you get all worked up. Let's hear what it's all about first.'

The woman looked grateful. 'You see, we were advised by the police to have him put down but, because we knew the circumstances, we felt – like this young lady here – that we ought to give him a chance. Such a lovely looking dog and only young.'

'He's all right, then. You haven't put him down, have you?' cried Alison, heart clenched so tight that it was a real pain in her chest.

'No, we haven't, but we have found a home for him elsewhere.'

'But he's my dog,' cried Alison. 'You can't give him to somebody else. He belongs to me.'

'I think it's just as well,' said Mum, sounding relieved. 'I'm sure he's got a very good home and he'll be very happy and that's that. We don't have to worry any more.'

Alison was too choked inside to say anything. Mum's words didn't sound real.

Uncle Reg said, 'Who's got him?'

'We've had a very nice man come up here several times looking for a dog to guard his workshop. A used-car dealer. He had a dog from us before but it had an accident. Very unfortunate. He was very upset about it. And when this dog came in, it seemed an ideal solution. So we gave him a ring and asked him to come along and see what he thought.'

'And Wolf went with him, just like that?' Alison could hardly breathe. She was beginning to shake.

'He was glad to get out of here. All the dogs are. They all want someone to love them.'

114

'Well, that's lovely.' Mum's sigh of relief was audible. 'Come on, Alison. He'll be all right. And when we get settled we can think about you having a dog then. That'll be nice, won't it?'

Tears blurred Alison's eyes. She couldn't bear to have anyone see them. Somehow she found herself outside the office, the damp air clinging to her hot face. She took gulping breaths which broke from her in moans.

'Oh, Jason, how right you are,' she found herself thinking. 'Caring just isn't enough.'

Mum and Uncle Reg were married just a few weeks later. There was nothing very special about the registry office wedding. Gran didn't come. Alison didn't know if Mum had invited her. Mum was more bothered about buying the right outfit, and worrying about the weather, than who was actually coming. Her friends from work were there, and some of Uncle Reg's friends, too, and they had a party at a pub and did a lot of laughing.

Alison started to call Uncle Reg 'Dad'. He had a semi-detached house with a garage and a big garden at the back, and Mum very soon started making things neat and tidy. Dad told Alison he didn't mind, as long as she kept out of the garage and left the muddle there alone. Alison had never lived in a house with a garden, and when she saw this garden – which wasn't very well set out because Dad wasn't much of a gardener and said he preferred things to look natural, anyway – all she could do was think how lovely it would have been to share it with Wolf.

She hadn't talked about Wolf since that day at the kennels. What was there to say? Mum didn't understand, anyway, and she had too many other things on her mind. Once or twice Dad had said to her, 'Still thinking about him?' and she had nodded and turned away before he could say any more. She could bear it if she didn't have to talk about him.

Every night in bed she would wonder how Wolf was getting on in his new home. It was very hard to have to think this way, and it brought tears to her eyes. Did Wolf like being a guard dog? Did the man really look after him?

Uncle Reg said the S.P.C.A. were very fussy before they allowed anyone to take a dog away, and kept a check on them afterwards, too. But did that man know what a lovely dog Wolf really was? Did Wolf live in his house or was he kept in the yard, in a kennel? Did anyone love him at all, or groom him, or take him for walks?

At first she had thought about trying to find Wolf, and go to see him. She said this to Uncle Reg but he told her it wasn't a good idea. It would only make Wolf unhappy.

'When you love somebody, or something, you've got to think about what's best for them, not what you want,' he told her. 'Love is knowing when to give up, as well as when to hold on.'

Knowing when to give up. That was dreadfully hard to learn because Alison wasn't very good at giving up, not when she wanted something badly enough. There had been in her life so few things that she really wanted. Wolf was the most important of them, and not to be able to have him was very hard.

One day she had been tempted to throw away Wolf's grooming kit but, after a struggle, she packed it in a box with her other things. You couldn't get rid of memories that easily, but she was glad when at last they moved to the new house, because she wouldn't have to go by Mrs Bailey's windows any more.

It was easier not to think about Wolf in her new surroundings, with so many new things to get used to as well as a new daily routine. It was strange not having a paper round; even stranger having breakfast with Dad every day, and then him taking her to school in his car on the way to work. They got to know each other a lot better on those short morning trips.

116

The weather was suddenly glorious and everybody started working in the garden. Mum wasn't much good. She kept pulling up flowers instead of weeds and couldn't see the difference even when Dad explained about six times. In the end she gave up trying and sat in a deck chair in a swimsuit, trying to restore her lost Greek tan.

One Saturday afternoon Alison was digging round the roots of some rose bushes, trying not to shudder when she turned up a centipede or stabbed a worm by mistake. Dad was mowing the lawn and when he finished he came to watch her.

'Of course, if we had a dog I don't suppose it'd be any good worrying too much about a nice garden,' he said.

Alison looked up at him in surprise, but he went on as if not noticing. 'It'd soon be a mess with a dog. Aren't they always supposed to be burying their bones somewhere? They do in cartoons, anyway.'

She didn't know why he was talking like this and she didn't know what to say. Was he thinking of getting her another dog? Had he talked to Mum about it? She hadn't said anything. But Alison didn't want another dog if she couldn't have Wolf, and she began to feel indignant inside. Did he really think she had forgotten Wolf already?

Tears prickled behind her eyes and she looked down hurriedly, not wanting him to know.

'I was thinking about Wolf,' he said to the back of her head.

'What?'

It was a mumble. She couldn't look up. She just dug away with the trowel, not knowing what she was doing as he went on talking.

'I had a phone call at work yesterday, you see. That man who took Wolf from the kennels. I didn't tell you I'd had a word with him before. Didn't want to upset you if I couldn't do anything. It'd only have made things worse. But I did try to get Wolf for you then, only he wasn't interested. He'd taken a fancy to him and wanted to keep him.'

Alison looked up at him, astonished, forgetting the tears on her cheeks. The sun was in her eyes and she couldn't see Dad properly, except that he was looking pleased with himself. Her mind was still blank.

'Why didn't you tell me?' she demanded.

'It wouldn't have helped much. He said no, and that seemed to be that. But, well . . .'

Alison was on her feet now, excited, anguished, clinging to him as she cried, 'What? What? Tell me!'

'Well, he rang up yesterday and said did I want Wolf because he just hadn't settled down there and wasn't going to be any good as a guard dog anyway. Just moping and not caring about anything, and off his food and all that.'

'You mean, I can have him after all? He's going to be mine? I don't believe it. Really? But what about Mum?'

The words just poured out. Alison didn't know if she was laughing or crying. They both turned to look at Mum. Her face was half hidden behind a pair of enormous sun glasses. She was asleep.

'I spent half of last night convincing her, but she's said yes. She said we've got to keep him in the garage, but we can have him.'

Alison flung her arms around Dad. He pretended to stagger backwards, laughing.

'When can we go and get him? When? When?'

'I said we'd be round there about half past six tonight.'

'What! But we haven't any food for him or anything. We haven't got anything ready.'

'Well, if you don't want to go, we'll leave it for another day.'

'No we won't,' Alison cried, bewildered, dizzy. 'Oh gosh! Gosh! I just can't believe it's true. Are you sure I'm not dreaming? I just can't believe it. Is Mum coming with us?'

118

'No. We're going out tonight and she takes two hours to get ready. You know that. We'll leave you to get Wolf settled in. We can call in at a pet shop on the way, before they shut.'

None of it seemed real to Alison. She couldn't believe that Wolf was going to be hers. She felt almost sick with excitement. Dad bought a really big basket for Wolf to sleep in, the biggest in the pet shop, as well as a huge bag of dog biscuits and a big block of frozen meat.

'Anything else we need?' he asked Alison, and she knew he was almost as excited about having Wolf as she was. There was a book in the shop about German Shepherd dogs and he bought that, too.

'Might as well find out all about them,' he said. 'Sounds like this Wolf is quite a dog.'

'Oh, he is,' she agreed. 'You'll see. He's the loveliest dog in the world.'

It was a half-hour drive to the man's address and twice Dad lost his way among the maze of streets and closely built houses, before they found the place they were looking for – adding to Alison's excitement and anguish. The used-car lot had high wooden fencing round it, but the gates were still open and a couple of men were wandering about, looking at cars. There was a wooden hut at one end of the yard on which someone had painted the words, 'All inquiries'. Wolf was nowhere in sight.

'Stay here,' said Dad. 'I'll go and inquire.'

He came to the door of the hut a minute later and beckoned to Alison. As she came up to the door he said, 'Just take a look in there.'

Alison put her head round the door. There was a desk and a man sitting there. There was a smell of grease and rust and cigarette smoke. There was a filing cabinet and, between the cabinet and the back wall, was a space where a dog lay half asleep, head on the floor between his paws. It was Wolf.

What a reunion that was! Afterwards Dad told Mum he wished he'd had a movie camera to take a permanent record of it. But then he would have needed sound, too, to capture all Wolf's yelps and whimpers and barks of joy, to join up with the way he jumped in the air, and slobbered all over Alison's face, and pawed her and knocked papers over the floor with his tail and had everybody laughing and Alison almost crying.

All the way home in the back seat of the car, Wolf panted and dripped saliva over Alison's hands and down her neck. He kept whining and dancing about and waving his tail, and all both Dad and Alison could do was grin and laugh and keep saying, 'Down, Wolf. Keep still. Don't get so worked up,' and so on, which he didn't take any notice of at all.

It was all too good to be true, yet it was true. And Wolf was the same as ever with Alison. He hadn't forgotten her for a moment. He was as pushy and bouncy as if they had never been separated.

Mum looked at him very warily, but admitted that he was rather a good-looking sort of dog.

'Got a pedigree as long as your arm,' Dad told her encouragingly. 'We'll be winning prizes with him yet.'

'You're as bad as Alison,' she replied.

'I don't really have to keep him in the garage, do I?' Alison pleaded, determined to have her own way. She couldn't bear to be parted from Wolf in such a way.

'He's a good guard dog,' said Dad, backing her up. 'You wouldn't have to worry about Alison being on her own when we go out, with a dog like that in the house.'

Mum couldn't argue against both of them. In the end she let Alison put Wolf's basket in the bedroom, and even found an old blanket for Wolf to sleep on. It was getting

120

late and she didn't want to waste any more time. She was dressed up to go dancing and the easiest thing was to give in.

When Alison and Wolf were alone it was like old times together. Wolf was as excited as she was and kept whimpering and barking and pushing his head against her, as if he could never tire of telling her how happy he was.

He did look a bit thin, but apart from a greasy smell about him, he was clean and in good condition. Alison took him out to the back garden, where he had a good sniff round and started digging up some flowers Dad had just planted. Alison dragged him away. She brought out his grooming kit and brushed and combed him from head to tail, remembering the times she had done this on the balcony outside Mrs Bailey's flat. It all seemed such a long time ago.

Wolf's dark eyes stared at her adoringly and his tail never stopped waving for a moment. Whenever he had the opportunity, his tongue slobbered over her face.

Then Alison clipped the lead on his collar and took him for a walk round the houses. She'd never bothered to explore the area before, but with a dog it was different. You found all sorts of interesting back alleys and other places that Wolf found quite fascinating. He made a couple of cats go stiff with fear and, in spite of his eagerness to discover every scent and turning, he constantly looked up at Alison, big jaws open, eyes adoring, as if he himself couldn't believe that they were together again.

When they came home, Alison put on the television for a while and Wolf sat on the sofa with her. Alison looked at Wolf and he looked at her, neither of them interested in the programme, both perfectly content.

When Alison went to bed, Wolf sniffed the basket that had been bought for him. He sat in it for a minute or two, as if to take possession of it, but as soon as Alison got into bed he jumped up to be with her.

Very half-heartedly Alison told him to get down, to go back to his basket, but Wolf didn't think much of sleeping on floors or in baskets when there was a good human bed he could share. He wriggled to just where he wanted to be, squashing Alison up against the wall, and with a sigh of contentment rested his long black muzzle in the crook of her arm.

Alison switched out the light. She didn't think she could bear any more happiness that day.

She began to remember the first time Wolf had slept on her bed, and then she couldn't help remembering all that had happened afterwards. She wondered if things would have turned out differently if she hadn't kept Wolf with her all that rainy weekend.

Was it really Wolf's constant whining and barking, and the neighbours banging on the walls and making threats, that had driven Mrs Bailey to do something so dreadful, or were there other things that Alison didn't know about and never would? Would Mrs Bailey still be alive if Alison hadn't first seen Wolf at the window, staring out so hopelessly day after day?

They were questions she couldn't answer. They scared her. They hurt.

Had Wolf forgotten Bobby by now, after all the things that had happened? Was there some part of him that would always remember? And what about Bobby? Would he one day forget Wolf, and Mrs Bailey, and everyone else? Would everyone forget about him? It was so strange. Bobby was only a name. Alison didn't even know what he looked like. Now, only Wolf would know him, if he didn't forget.

Thinking like this hurt far too much. She reached out for Wolf and felt his wet nose and warm muzzle and another little wriggle of contentment from him. He was there, safe and comforting, willing to love her without question, and she could sleep because she had what she wanted.

But just then she knew that Wolf wasn't everything. She had her heart's desire, but there was pain in it because of all the things she could do nothing about. How did you learn to live with those things? Perhaps tomorrow she would find out.